THE REST
IS SILENCE

Published by Dwyer Editions

Author's website
www.kevin-scully.com

Kevin Scully has asserted his right under
the Copyright, Designs and Patents Act 1988
to be identified as the author of this work

ISBN 978-1-84396-554-1

Also available as a Kindle ebook
ISBN 978-1-84396-555-8

A catalogue record for this book
is available from the British Library and
the American Library of Congress.

While this book contains some real names
and places, it has to be stressed that all events are
purely fictional, perhaps even those
relating to the Editor.

Cover design by Dennis Adelman/Menace Graphics
menacegraphicsltd@gmail.com

Typesetting and pre-press production
eBook Versions
27 Old Gloucester Street
London WC1N 3AX
www.ebookversions.com

By the same author

Fiction
Harbour Glimpses

Non-Fiction
Sensing the Passion
Women on the Way
Into Your Hands
Five Impossible Things
to Believe Before Christmas
Imperfect Mirrors
Simple Gifts
Three Angry Men

More information can be found at
www.kevin-scully.com

About the author

Kevin Scully is the author of a range of published and performed works. They include one novel, *Harbour Glimpses*. His non-fiction includes *Sensing the Passion*, *Women on the Way*, *Into Your Hands*, *Imperfect Mirrors*, *Five Impossible Things to Believe Before Christmas* and *Simple Gifts*.

His radio dramas *Verbal Assaults* and *A Grain of Rice* were broadcast in Australia and Ireland respectively.

Ten works, including *There's One in Every Unit*, *The Glint of the Irish* and *Hard Up* have been seen on stage in the United Kingdom and Australia.

His short stories won a number of awards and some of his poems have been published.

Three Angry Men, a spiritual memoir of his father, Ken, who was also known by his pen name John Dawes, is available through his website, www.kevin-scully.com.

Kevin is a former journalist, with experience in newspapers, television and radio. He trained as an actor at the National Institute of Dramatic Art in Sydney and worked professionally on the stage, film, television and radio for ten years.

He is a priest in the Church of England and is married to the opera singer Adey Grummet.

THE REST IS SILENCE

Kevin Scully

DWYER EDITIONS

The Beginning of an End

Father Aidan the Abbot is going down to die. If and when he does, the monastic order to which he has given his life will die too. I am going to die with him. Yet it is likely, too—unless God has plans for me that I cannot discern—that I will survive him. Even so, when he leaves this life, my life—at least in the religious sense—will come to an end as well. Because I will be the only member left of the Community of Saint Candida. And a community cannot consist of one. Or can it?

Yet what will I be? My vows will still stand but who will oversee them? I will be permanently cut loose from my brethren. Can I renounce the CSC? Perhaps I should ask our Visitor. But, as a bishop, he is distracted by allegations of sexual impropriety of a parish priest in his diocese. Would he want to continue as Visitor when Father Aidan and I move from Dorset to London? Or would he transfer our oversight to a local wearer of purple? And no matter who takes on the role, a similar question remains: can you be a Visitor to a community of one?

Is it possible to resume the life of a man cast aside nearly fifty years ago? Though even then I did not cease to be who I was. I became a new man, with a new name, a member of a

1

community in which an individual finds meaning as a brother, but still with all the baggage I brought with me. Should I abandon this identity, whose name is Brother Columba, assumed in 1972? Even the name was part of a collective process. It was chosen for me by Brother Anthony, the Novice Master of the order, at my profession.

'You were washed up here in a wheelbarrow much as Columba was washed up at Iona in his coracle. You would do well to aspire to a life of service like his,' he said.

So Columba it was. I had hoped that I could opt for the Irish form of the name, Colmcille, but Father Abbot, to whom I had appealed for the equivalent of a deed poll change of name in religion, was adamant. 'If you are returning to your English roots, the Anglicised name will be enough.'

Father Aidan was already an experienced, or so it seemed to me, member of the monastery on my arrival— yet well in advance of his being elected abbot. He had been professed fifteen years earlier, having given up his academic career—recusant Catholicism in the Elizabethan era was his specialism—to take to the cloister. Even then he was still sought after as an external academic supervisor, a task which Father Abbot both sanctioned and rationed. He took the view that it would keep Aidan abreast of developments and bring in some useful income to the community.

But things move on. And now it was come for us, the last two members of our order, to move on with them. The plans had been made by the Trustees who constitute the Management Committee of our community. This mixture of religious and secular great and good, with Father Abbot being the community presence, had overseen the exit strategy. This would solve the challenge of meeting bills for a vast set of buildings in a large rural setting. The plant was being sold off—something agreed to but not engineered by the Abbot when he was clear in mind (something that he is now, sadly, not) —and the proceeds would support the dying number of us—we happy two—until we die.

And so I find myself sitting with Fr Aidan as we await our transport to Bethnal Green.

EDITOR'S NOTE

What you have just read comes from a pile of scribbled pages which had been stuffed into an envelope and handed to me at the front desk of Care Home, a facility I go to as part of my pastoral duties as Rector of the parish of St Matthew's, Bethnal Green.

It was given to me by the receptionist as I was on my way in to take a mass in the first floor lounge room, something another priest or I try to do each week. The envelope did not have my name on it. Indeed, it had no markings on it at all. I had a brief look at its contents. When I asked the woman behind the desk why she had given it to me, she said the manager of the home had told her to do so. I put the envelope and its contents into the bag which held the chalice, paten and other necessaries for the Eucharist I was on my way to celebrate.

The weekly Eucharist at Care Home was, and remains, a high point of my week. St Matthew's parish is rapidly, and sometimes bewilderingly, changing. The mass provides a still point in the turmoil of the world and especially so in the loosening minds of some residents of the home. Ritual can somehow reconnect otherwise lost elements of memory and culture. Hymns bring voices raised in joy and certitude, as does the recitation of the Lord's Prayer and the Hail Mary. As the officiating priest, one gets a sense of reintegration of fragmented parts of former lives. Such is the power of religion.

When I got back to my study I gave the contents of the envelope a more considered looking over. They were random jottings, thoughts and memories, from a monk who had been for a little over a year a resident in Care Home. As I scanned

4

them, I was struck by a sense of intrusion, that I was looking in on thoughts and events that should be kept private.

They were written, as you have read, by Columba CSC. (That stands for the Community of Saint Candida.) He had joined another monk, Fr Aidan, who had made a journey from rural Dorset to Bethnal Green. Columba tells us that Aidan had lived at the St Candida's Monastery since he withdrew from academe. Some years earlier he had left the East End of London, taking a circuitous route to Oxford where he read Theology, in which he gained a first, and then pressed on in research. A devout young man, forged by the great Anglo-Catholic revival in the inner city, rural Suffolk and Oxford, he decided to test a vocation to the monastic life. It clearly suited him but, as I came to learn, as other mental faculties degenerated, he developed almost a compulsion that he should die near where he was born. He got his wish thanks to those who oversaw the winding up of the monastery. And through the efforts and sacrifice of Brother Columba.

Columba is the last of a line. When he dies—after Fr Aidan's death he moved from Care Home to the clergy retirement centre of Lazarus House in Sussex—so will the community of which he has been a professed member since 1972. I asked Columba why the two of them had not moved directly to Sussex when the monastery closed. He said it was Aidan's wish and, since Fr Aidan was still abbot (despite his fading mental grip), he felt he must honour it. I questioned the wisdom of that. Columba's response was that I did not live under a vow of obedience.

I made contact with Columba at Lazarus House; indeed, I have been to visit him a number of times. I miss his quietly supportive contributions to our weekly mass at Care Home, and his prayerful presence at our Sunday services. I have repeatedly offered to return his jottings. He doesn't want them back. They were, he tells me, merely attempts to pass the time, essays to avoid the constant buzz of television and radio, in the home where he was effectively an additional unpaid carer. This was to Aidan mostly but, by virtue of his clarity of mind, he was also something of an advocate for other residents. He was one of only a few on his floor who did not live with dementia.

He has approved of my making them public, on certain conditions, though he has given me precious little steerage as to the sequence in which they should be presented. When I asked him for some such assistance, he simply shrugged and said there was no hierarchy of thought in them. Nor could he tell me if he had written his personal memories in sequence. They were undated as to writing or record, so any chronology was guess work. The order is simply my following a hunch or a failed attempt to construct some artifice. Any fault in this is entirely my own. I have also tried to refrain from too much comment—though sometimes I have struggled with this, as I do in much of life.

Columba's memories, in spite of their appeal, are not always accurate in fact and sequence. Research has confirmed that, but I have decided not to take issue with his narrative and comments. At times he repeats himself. Such rumination is normal, if not very literary. But to edit out the repetitions would be to sacrifice some other revelation or thought that flows from them. I simply offer what he has to say. There are also inconsistencies in his use of capitals for words like Community, when referring to the Order—or order—of which he was a professed member. I have left such variations in their original form.

He also has a habit of referring to fellow monks by the posts they held at the time—Fr Abbot, Guestmaster, Novice Master, Prior, Brother Garden, Brother Kitchen, Infirmarian, Sacristan, Librarian. At other times, particularly in reference to his novitiate, he uses Christian names of those 'in the world', as monastics say. It is potentially confusing as any given incident, depending on what Columba recalls, may have occurred with the same person in various roles or under different names. This is particularly true of abbots.

I have, where I have felt it useful, made some notes, often relating to embedded scriptural references in Columba's writing. I have also sought to unravel some of Columba's personal, historical and religious elements that may elude the casual reader. This has been done in the form of footnotes. I do this gingerly, having been entranced by Anthony Grafton's 'curious history' of the footnote. As it says on the book's dustcover, 'Like the toilet, the modern footnote is essential to civilized historical life; like the toilet, it seems a poor subject for civil conversation, and attracts attention, for the most part, when it malfunctions. Like the toilet, the footnote enables one to deal with ugly tasks in private; like the toilet, it is tucked genteelly away—often, in recent years, not even at the bottom of the page, but at the end of the book. Out of sight, even out of mind, seems exactly where so banal a device belongs'.[1]

There were also random notes, torn from other pieces of paper—notebooks, newspapers, scraps —on which were sayings, jottings, thoughts, comments, quotations and recollections. These present a greater challenge and so I have sought to do no more than place them within the body of the papers as it appealed to me. There was no key to how they related to the rest of the material. Their placement is pure whim on my part.

Some aspects of them are possibly shocking, one incident extremely so. But, as a fellow Christian (and an Australian-born one at that), I believe Columba's disjointed narrative points to a truth about ourselves—no matter how unpleasant events, experience or thoughts are, they are facts of life. To attempt to alter them would be dishonest. I offer them because they chronicle something of the dying landscape of the Church of England in the early part of the twenty-first century.

1. Anthony Grafton, *The Footnote*, Faber and Faber Limited, London, 1997.

The Water's Edge

Bensville was a paradise. How my parents chose this glorious, isolated place was a mystery to me. It was quiet, its stillness sometimes reflected in the unruffled morning surface of Brisbane Water. Perhaps this is where the seed of silence in my life was sown. It germinated, as did my life itself, thousands of miles away. Then it was an unwelcome gift—fraught with fear and possibility, something which I only wanted to flee.

The Central Coast hamlet was remote, especially by road. Travel was mostly by boat. It was leisurely, but more swift than relying on irregular bus services. I foolishly thought I had outgrown its confines. Later in life I found freedom in so many restrictions, often imposed in silence. There, in a world where green met blue, I was unknowingly readying myself for the community that I now lead in everything but title.

The other isolating factor was my age. It seemed there were only two of us under the age of twenty—Marian and me. I thought our parents ancient. They weren't, as I now know. They must have been considerably younger than most of Bensville's other residents, who had retired seemingly to fish and garden themselves towards death.

We each took the Pioneer ferry that my father polited on

behalf of the Sisters of St Joseph, who ran an orphanage at South Kincumber, a short haul across the water from Bensville, also known locally as Sunnyside.

My father would go down the wharf—or should I write The Wharf, it being the centre of our community?—his handmade wooden box holding the magneto over his shoulder, place the device into the shaft, put a leather strap over a raised stud on the flywheel, pull, and kick the engine into life, then chug over the bay to collect the ferry.

On board Dad would make the rounds to various bays and inlets, collecting passengers, parcels, papers and post on the way to the glittering Woy Woy, where he would exchange his cargo for that which had made its way up the coast on the train from Sydney or down from Newcastle. On the return trip shopkeepers, newsagents, postmasters and assorted locals would await him on jetties servicing the small communities that gorged on freshly caught fish and sunshine. His ultimate destination was the orphanage.

Sometimes a nun would be going to or from the convent at the start, or end, of a retreat. Other, older women would be sent on respite for or from the houses they shared with other members of the order. There was also the occasional corpse in a coffin to go to the train at Woy Woy. Or he would collect one for burial at one of the hamlets into which he called.

Then there was the human cargo which was very much alive—a child on his way to join the ranks of the unwanted, unplanned or unloved at the orphanage. As these children reached their teens, they would need to be relocated. Some went into trades locally, though this was a limited opportunity, or were sent north to Newcastle or south to Sydney for placement in positions considered commensurate with their academic or industrial prowess. A number popped up on ferries in Sydney, having honed their skills on Brisbane Water. A lot got apprenticeships with the railways or the steelworks. A few went to university. A couple achieved fame in the performing arts, graduates of the orphanage Wonder Band. A surprising number opted to enter the religious life. How many of them stayed the course, I don't know.

I have not seen the institution since the funeral of my parents, which took place in St Paul's Church of England, some distance from the orphanage. Both mum and dad were killed in a road accident in my father's first car. I had moved to Sydney by then. As soon as I had settled up their estate, I decided to quit the country.

EDITOR'S NOTE

Reading of Bensville was a shock. There was nothing in Columba's voice that betrayed his Australian upbringing to me, though a number of residents at Care Home told me they had picked it up. Eastenders have a good ear for this—they have often commented on a tinge of a twang in my tones.

Bensville is a waterside hamlet—a tiny place at the time Columba is referring to—on the Central Coast of New South Wales. I had come to know it fairly well. My parents had bought a holiday house there in the early 1970s. It was a fantastically beautiful place, with the colours and dangers Columba later describes.

The fibro cottage, Karinya, was built with an obstinate inversion. Its front door faced away from the panoramic views to be had from the glassed in back verandah which, in denial of the atmospherics, had windows that could not be opened onto the breeze off the water. It was the resort of the family holiday, the weekend, the half-term break. It also brought attendant duties, such as mowing the grass which grew at greater speeds than that at our Sydney home in suburban Campsie, no doubt helped by the seepage from a septic tank.

It was later the venue of many surfing weekends. A couple of cars and vans, with boards strapped to the roof, full of hard drinking late-teenagers, would wind their way up the old roads towards Gosford. The toll was to be avoided at all costs. We would head towards the waves on the coast, a favourite but sometimes dangerous climb up Wards Hill Road from Empire Bay, along the flat towards Maitland Bay, before dropping down to the idyllic Macmasters Beach, with its waterfront car park and café.

Over the years the natural beauty diminished, as it will by the incursions of any sustained building and development that will ultimately destroy the flora and fauna that make a landscape distinctive. I would return to visit my parents every couple of years and more of the beauty was replaced by costly but aesthetically questionable edifices.

On one visit my mother Norma warned me I would be unhappy, only to put me in a car—we could have walked—and drove me around the streets of a clear-felled concreted wasteland where exotic plants popped up in isolation. McMansions with long sweeping drives terminated in triple garages. It was all Robin Boyd's *Australian Ugliness* writ in hard standing.

All attempts to draw Columba to discuss the village were fruitless. I had learned that he was polite but circumspect. I wanted to question him as so much of the place I recognised from his writings: the tracks, the boatsheds, the wharf, the colourful and at times dangerous wildlife. There were facts I wanted to clarify. (Facts hound me. Perhaps it is my journalistic background: my wife says I won't even let someone tell a humorous anecdote uninterrupted if there is an error.)

But, as with much of his disconnected writings, I have had to let it go. For Columba could well have used the words ascribed to Pontius Pilate, *quod scripsi, scripsi.*[1] Indeed, I have probably written too much of my own experience here. Columba's story, however fragmentary, is much more interesting.

1. 'What I have written, I have written'—John 19:21.

Growing Pains

It seemed that everyone in Bensville was retired. That could not have been so. My father worked the ferry. My mother wrote romantic stories for the Women's Weekly and, under a pseudonym for its competitor, Woman's Day. Her published efforts made their way to our house through my father's work. I was not encouraged to read them.

'There is stuff worth reading. And stuff that is done to put food on the table. You will learn to tell the difference,' she once said as she took the Women's Weekly from my hands.

It was an adult world and I was the only boy. There was one other child, Marian. Her parents must have been about the same age as mine. Her presence meant we were destined to be friends. Time together was a mixture of comfort and tension, all that two strong personalities could foment. One repeated compromise to difference was skipping. One end of the rope would be tied to the gatepost, the other person—the one not 'in'—would turn the rope and chant the rhyme:

Cinderella
dressed in yella
went downstairs

to meet her fella.
On the way
her panties busted;
how many people
were disgusted?

Peppers, those jealousy-fed speeding circles of rope, with rapid counting to accompany them, 'One, two, three, four, five...' I learned many girls' games, though in our isolation they did not feel especially feminine. They were just part of the landscape we inhabited.

In the same way our 'adventures' did not feel especially masculine or feminine—the shoreline foraging for oysters, our secretive explorations to the uncharted territory beyond the boatshed, the imaginative narratives that accompanied them, the cubby houses built under the canopy of lantana. It was in one such hidey-hole that I got my first kiss and, never to be repeated as little ones, a glimpse of her private parts in return for an exhibition of my own.

We would go to Woy Woy each morning on the ferry where, by virtue of our differing ages, gender and, more importantly, denomination, we attended different schools. She would go off the school run by the same order of nuns who lived across the bay and ran the orphanage. I would go to the public school.[1]

As adolescence took hold—it became apparent to each and the other—our adventures took a new course. Being the solitary representative of the opposite sex in the same age group meant there was no distraction or discussion outside school. My journey across the water continued, though the destination changed—Woy Woy High. Marian would walk up Kallaroo Road to Empire Bay Road, to collect the semi-trailer-like bus that took her to the Catholic girls' school in East Gosford. On return, homework and parents permitting, we would seek each other out.

The colours of the waterside hamlet faded in the glare of the luminosity of our changing bodies. So much had sparkled until then. The mix of yellow, green, blue and white of the budgerigars; the alternative presentations of the rosella—the entire prism or the strident red and blue; the soft grey and pink of a galah; the various tans and beige of the kookaburra; the yellow flash on the alert head of a cockatoo.

Even dangers were colour coded. First up were the snakes: red on the belly of the black snake (and its mistakenly attributed name to its cousin with the yellow underside); the dark brown, the most vicious of all; and the black and gold of the spectacular tiger. Some of the rainbow made it to spiders too: the giant Nephila and, lurking danger to all hurriedly putting their bums on the seat of an outside toilet, the redback.

We were constantly warned to be on our guard for these and other hidden dangers—ticks, poisonous plants, jagged rocks and dangerous tree roots—but familiarity breeds complacency if not contempt.

Besides, we were changing. As hair sprouted on my upper and nether parts, my voice broke. Marian shot up in height as her chest filled outwards. Alone and together we were more aware of ourselves and each other. The colours around us and their attendant dangers faded.

New ones arose. My centre of consciousness moved south from my brain to my groin. Confusing pleasures came with unsought erections. Stroking gave me satisfaction but the very existence of a taut member gave me a self-conscious pride.

Alone, I would strip, and bend a school ruler along the side of my member, carefully noting its length and width, and being bewilderingly proud of its sturdiness. I would hang shirts and other clothing, even towels, from it. I was absorbed by the tension that nothing, short of stimulation to ejaculation, would release.

Marian and my hitherto innocent excursions became less explorations of place than of person. Boat trips went from being from fishing expeditions to quests for an isolated spot where we would tie up the boat and go ashore. Our incursions into each other became increasingly adventurous. Gentle external stimulation was overtaken by lifting up of cloth, testing of elastic, unclasping of fixtures to grasp, grab and poke what our fingers encountered. Once I heard my own gasp as I found my way to her pubic area, gently explored a moisture that pushed my hardness beyond control. Hours later I lay on board the drifting dinghy, luxuriating in the smell of Marian on my unwashed hand.

These journeys reached their apogee one evening. Having informed our parents that we were going out to look out at the water from the wharf, we allowed ourselves to be seen by some of the men with their fishing lines adrift in the dying light. We struck off into the track, skipped into the bush and imagined ourselves hidden and out of earshot behind a boatshed. Astonishment took hold of my mind as Marian unbuttoned my trousers, slipped down my underpants, knelt on the ground, and then without a hint of overture, placed her mouth around my penis.

Years of experience, shame and prayer have not erased the amazement as Marian tightened her teeth around me, causing an instant eruption, and her seeming wide eyed wonder as she gazed up at me, taking everything from my pulsating frame. She held me till I was flaccid then, without a word, stood up, put a finger to her lips and walked back towards Kallaroo Road, leaving me to recover.

The next day I saw Marian's mother coming down the path to our house. Always a voluble visitor, this time she was taciturn. I was despatched by my mother to do some gardening while the two women had a prolonged chat over a proverbial cup of tea. Chores in the shed were similarly found for me when my father later strode up from the wharf and went into the house.

My father's interview with me was circumspect. I was becoming a man. Some things were difficult. The word 'gentleman' meant we should behave properly. A gentleman knew the meaning of restraint. I returned a vacant look. 'Look, son,' Dad snapped. 'Marian is out of bounds from now on. You're both venturing into dangerous waters.'

A couple of weeks later Marian's family moved to the peninsula. I saw her on her way home from school until the move, but that was it. We never found ourselves alone together again. So there was no opportunity to mention our exploratory past.

When they left I found myself drifting around the village—to the wharf, to the shop, into the bush, to the newly emptied house, and to the scene of the extraordinary event that somehow led to the curtailment of our relationship.

It is a long time ago and much has happened in both our lives. I ponder, as I am sure many do in similar circumstances, if she has ever given any thought to that amazing evening that stymied our contact and friendship. I have never been able to erase that locking of our eyes as I released myself into her mouth. I had no words at the time, and have found none since.

1. Columba's reference to a public school is essentially an Australian one, i.e. in the state system. It is not to be confused with the elitist English institutions that falsely parade under the same name.

The Novice Master was very keen on the Salve Regina. He seemed particularly moved when we would get to the bit about the 'vale of tears'. The Prior, in one of his occasional addresses to the novices, happened to say that he felt some of our faith—and the prayers we knew and loved—erred too much on the side of pain and failure. I looked over towards the Novice Master but his face was impassive. At the time this view from a senior brother seemed reassuringly sensible. It has stayed with me. So much joy; so much to be thankful for.

Feed my Sheep

I don't where this came from. Or why. But I was watching something on the television with Fr Abbot—he likes to watch anything, as do many of our fellow residents here at Care Home—when an old episode of *One Man and His Dog* came on. This had passed me by. Not surprisingly, I suppose, as I was never really much of a television viewer. Less so when I joined community.

Yet watching the man (Welsh) and his dog (a Border Collie) and his sheep (Border Leicester) led to a cascade of memories. My parents had bought an Arthur Mee's Encyclopaedia as a present for my birthday—I can't remember which one, but obviously I was able to read it unassisted. Reading was part and parcel of life at home. My mother's writing absorbed her. Every now and then I would be shooed out of the house so she could finish a story or meet a deadline.

My father brought in books from the library at Woy Woy, or those sent by magazines for my mother to review. There was a stream into the house of magazines, from the highbrow to those from which my mother earned a living. The linen press, kitchen cabinets, the bathroom cupboard—at least one shelf of these would be given over to literature. It was some years before my father yielded to the inevitable and built my mother some bookshelves for her library. It was only then order could first be established and then maintained. Woe betide either of the males in the house if they disrupted her library. Pride of place, of course, went to three books: the dictionary, the complete works of Shakespeare and the Pears Cyclopaedia. This latter work was replaced every year, the superseded volume being relegated to its chronological place on the second shelf. It was on the bottom shelf of this bookcase that Arthur Mee was stored.

We had not yet run to a television. Even when we did we needed an aerial that was nearly twenty foot high. The ten volumes of the encyclopaedia were just the ticket for my father, who would reminisce about life in the Old Country, and for me, who would absorb (and rapidly forget) many alarming and interesting facts. Dad would often take a volume off to bed to read. Of course, Mr Mee had included nothing that would disturb or upset a young mind. But he did provide in his ten volumes a treasure trove of knowledge, oddities and history cast in the Old Imperial Ways.

A couple of pages of photographs of sheep caught my eye. It was through this I became something of an unchallenged expert on breeds I rarely got to see. There were not many sheep in the Bensville area—those areas of bush that had been cleared were mostly given over to dairy farming—and the ones I did encounter were invariably were Australian Merinos, believed to be the result of genetic modification, known more innocently as cross-breeding, of John Macarthur. Though revisionists have suggested that this is to do down the efforts of his wife, Elizabeth. The history (re-)writers say that he was so busy in the political life of the early colony—and later with his own delusions, by reason of insanity—that he did not really have time to supervise animal husbandry. Like many women in many fields, Elizabeth's efforts were apportioned to her spouse and thus her claim to fame was robbed of her. Even to the point of his being pictured with a sheep on the first two dollar note. (I don't recall the Macarthurs having a listing in Arthur Mee's Encyclopaedia.)

Wanting a more robust animal for the Australian conditions, and one that would produce a good clip, using rams from Spain, along with ewes from various other breeds, a new strain of Merino was developed. Fleeces from New South Wales found their place in the wool market. I came to learn—another mystery of accumulated trivia that clogs my mind—that there are a number of varieties that parade under the title Australian Merino. (I did not get that from Arthur Mee.)

But back in the home country there were plenty of breeds growing wool. And it was these which were photographed and displayed in Arthur Mee's Encyclopaedia. As I said, I would pore over the pictures. Then, as a test, I would cover the caption line and set out to indentify the animals: Beltex, Cheviot, Corriedale, Dorper, Romney Marsh, Hampshire Down.

When I started travelling around Britain, I found myself calling out breeds of sheep as I saw them, many for the first time, not on the page, but in the field. This was a grown-up-child's car game and it amused and perplexed my travelling companions. Donna was particularly entertained by this. I wonder if, among the bad memories I no doubt provided her with, she ever recalled this lighter aspect of our relationship.

When I came to St Candida's, I likewise amused myself on early exploratory walks, recalling this specialist knowledge, though most of the animals disappointingly turned out not to be Dorset Down but Suffolk.

Fr Scully, in one of his attempts to animate a particularly somnolent Eucharistic congregation, in a homily on the Good Shepherd, once told the story of an organist who, as the coffin was carried out of the church at the end of the funeral of a local butcher, played Bach's *Sheep May Safely Graze*. No breed was mentioned.

The Journey Gone

I had already booked my passage in the steerage of a Ten Pound Pom ship returning to England. Income from my parents' estate—I received royalties on my mother's stories which had been published in book form for some years along with a small pension—and my warehouseman's day job and weekend bar work at an RSL club[1] in Sydney provided both the requisite income and the exclusion of time to spend it. There was a tribe of us, working two or three jobs, stacking up the money like a bar handy's[2] glass stack, along with hopes to play it out for as long as we could when we got to Europe. We wanted to make every penny stretch as far as it could.

I had another secret card up my sleeve besides my relative wealth—a British passport because of my father, who had been born in Bermondsey. It was his experience as a lighterman that got him on to boats out on the Thames, war service in the Royal Navy, after which he worked his passage on a merchant ship to Australia, where he met and married my mother, and eventually found him piloting a ferry on the Brisbane Water.

We drank and played our way across the Pacific Ocean, with little indication as to our place in the world. A camaraderie developed in which our excesses and payment for them were part of the common account. Duty free booze was an enormous temptation to which we yielded too often. Even at the seemingly ridiculous prices, it could bite into savings. Unlike some of my fellow travellers, I was not going to act like a millionaire just because booze was cheap and there was little else to do. Which wasn't true. There was the pool, deck tennis, board games, even a library, but this seemed to pass by many of the younger passengers. For some the trip was a dual crossing, with liquid beneath the hull and in the person. There was a whole world awaiting us at Southampton and I wanted to be able to look around and live it up a bit when I got there.

Despite my financial acuity, I was in many ways an innocent. The easy way of men and women together revealed unimagined opportunities. Shipboard romances led to an establishment of codes—a tie over the door handle, a towel in the corridor, a look over the drink being handed to you— to alert us that one of our number was 'entertaining' in the four bunk cabins we shared in steerage. Privacy was gained by lottery. The one who fixed an assignation first had the right to the cabin, unless a prior arrangement had been made.

The journey extended my education and was the unravelling of my moral structure, such as it was. I was never very religious. Church attendance was something that was part of my family's life—my father somehow found a place to tie up his inboard motor boat in a cove near St Paul's, carry up his magneto, and still look presentable in a suit inside the oldest church on the coast. For all that, I realise now that I became relatively well versed in the Bible and church life. This was a testament to my parents, the local church and particularly those who came to our public school on Fridays to lead our scripture classes. Yet here was fun, the company of the unleashed and the untroubled, and it seemed churlish not to partake of the low-hanging fruit on offer.

I sought to make my encounters significant. For the most part I shared my erotic energy with one young woman who had done me the flattery of speaking of a range of aspirations for her future in England, the Continent and, even at the start of the adventure, of what she would do when she was back 'at home'. The invitation to her cabin was a surprise in itself. What followed was a revelation.

About a month into the trip I learned, by accident as she and one of my companions emerged from her cabin, that she was casting her net a little wider than me. In a mixture of excitement and pique I approached my friend's cast-off object of lustful affection in the bar that night. I was stunned and delighted to be welcomed with full privileges, as High Churchmen used to say.

That eased me into a broader, though hardly extensive, range of dalliance. The next fortnight allowed me to understand variety in sex was wider than I had ever imagined. It was, in many ways, the beginning of a decline which I repent of but, shamefully, on occasion still find some pleasure in recalling. I once saw a play in the West End—I cannot recall its name or author—in which former comrades-in-arms discuss their past. One sighs, slaps his thigh, looks up into the air and says, 'Ah yes. Great days. And great sins.[3]

All this took place as the ship moved into new and different climes and places. The changing, at times frightening, conditions at sea: sometimes a flat, glossy calm; the wind making its approach apparent in gentle, darkening patterns on the water; the albatross that hung over the stern of the boat, unperturbed by exhaust from the funnels, diving with alacrity on the food waste when it was thrown from the lower decks. And the storms in which even the well seasoned sailors seemed fearful. As well they should.[4]

And the ticking off of the ports—Wellington, where more rowdy travellers came on board, Punto Arena, Buenos Aires, Rio de Janeiro. A stunning, threatening, passage through the Straits of Magellan (you felt you could just lean over the rails of the ship and touch the cliffs as we passed).

Beauty, exotica and excitement were tinged by the reality of oppression. A number of places we embarked at were under military rule and that somehow—properly, I now think—dampened our spirits. It took a day or two before the party atmosphere was restored onboard.

By then we thought ourselves on the other side of the world, which to a bunch of Australians and New Zealanders, we were—Tenerife, Lisbon, Vigo, then Southampton. From there the train to a dim, foggy London.

These are, in some ways, my monastic antecedents. My dissolution continued on land. The travels and excursions in geography and flesh were unsustainable.

Thank God my excesses landed me in a hedge by St Candida's. Yet, even now, I wonder how I made the transition from accidental hedonist to monk. 'Love's redeeming work is done,' goes the hymn.[5] It refers, of course, to Jesus and his saving of the world. If one were presumptuous—as, indeed, anyone who professes faith has to be at some time—there is an extension: Love's redeeming work is being done. As it says in another hymn, 'My chains fell off and I was free.'[6]

---

1. Returned and Services League, the equivalent of the (Royal) British Legion.

2. An Australianism for someone who collects the empties in a pub or club.

3. Neither have I been able to source this play.

4. One of the random pieces of paper I found in the envelope left for me at Care Home had a transcription of the Coverdale version of Psalm 107:23-31. It could almost be inserted at this point:

They that go down to the sea in ships:
and occupy their business in great waters;
These men see the works of the Lord:
and his wonders in the deep.
For at his word the stormy wind ariseth:
which lifteth up the waves thereof.
They are carried up to the heaven, and down again to the deep:
their soul melteth away because of the trouble.
They reel to and fro, and stagger like a drunken man:
and are at their wit's end.
So when they cry unto the Lord in their trouble:
he delivereth them out of their distress.
For he maketh the storm to cease:
so that the waves thereof are still.
Then are they glad, because they are at rest:
and so he bringeth them unto the haven where they would be.
O that men would therefore praise the Lord for his goodness:
and declare the wonders that he doeth for the children of men!

5. By Charles Wesley.

6. *And Can It Be*, also by Charles Wesley.

Seeds in the Garden

This all came out wrong. Still, the progression of events is more or less accurate, inasmuch as I could ever remember it with clarity.[1]

The day broke like a box of eggs dropped onto the pavement. There was a sound of tearing canvas as I tried to look up. I was in no state to recognise anything. The light was too bright. I closed my eyes in the vain hope that by doing so the crashing ache in my head, in a place just behind my pupils, would evaporate.

A sound, far removed from the harshness of the piercing illumination, came to me.

'Oh dear.' A pause. 'Oh dear oh dear.'

I forced open my eyelids. I put my hand over my brow to make an inadequate shield.

'Oh dear oh dear oh dear.'

The reality of my circumstances began to emerge. I was by a hedgerow. My hair and face were speckled with dry vomit. I had been lucky enough to turn away from my emesis, saving myself from a rock and roll death. A crumpled sleeping and shoulder bag, their contents disgorged as a material echo of my stomach's, lay on the ground nearby. My wallet, passport and other valuables were in an ironically neat pile by my dishevelment.

I tried to sit up. Awareness of my physical state was immediate. The headache was life-threatening; my throat was parched; my eyes ached and were filled with what felt like sand.

'Oh dear, no. We can't have this. Can you stand up?'

Hands were placed under my armpits. I made a sound. I thought it was an affirmative response to the question. I threw up.

'Oh dear. We need you to get you to the house. You can't stay here.'

I closed my eyes. I must have dozed off. When I opened them again, with the same sensations that greeted the first attempt, I could make out two men in black robes. Hands were placed under my armpits again and I was grasped by my feet. I was swinging in the air. I was lowered into a curved shell, my head and feet dangling from different ends. There was an edge of metal behind my knees. A tugging at my feet brought my back on to a slight angle. A pillow was placed behind my head.

I looked to see my legs dangling between the handles of a large wheelbarrow. It was in this carriage that I made a bumpy and physically challenging—for both driver and passenger!— ride that ended at the Guesthouse of the Community of Saint Candida.

I was led to a bathroom.

'Can you undress yourself?' I grunted and shuffled off my clothes. Water was turned on and I stepped into an ocean of abrasive warmth. I gave myself a long, cleansing, guilt-ridden bath. I got out, rubbed myself down, chucked myself into the robe that had been left to me and was led by another black-clad man to a bed, into which I collapsed.

I am told I slept for twenty-seven hours. The Guestmaster

of the monastery would pop in occasionally to check on me. I had a clearing head, one good enough to ask the gentleman who handed me a small towel, soap, toothbrush and toothpaste, while giving me directions to the nearest bathroom, to ask on my return from my ablutions:

- where was I?
- what had happened to my Kombi van?
- who were the occasional men in black I saw?
- where was Donna?

'Hang on.' The man who had furnished me with toiletries put his hand up. A bell was tolling not too far away. 'I will be back in about twenty minutes.' With that he left.

I looked around. I was in a small, spartan, but comfortable room. The single bed was solid, with a mattress on the hard side. Not that I had noticed. There was a hanging rail, some open space between a lounge chair (upright, with wings to catch a nodding head) and a small wooden table-desk, with a simple wooden chair in front of it. Above the desk was a bookshelf. Over the bed's headboard was a crucifix.

Hang On returned with another man in black.

'Ah, you're up. Good. You look much better.' He extended his hand for me to shake. 'I am Father Martin. And this is Brother Kentigern. I am the one who found you. Do you remember?'

I made some vague response.

'It is time for lunch,' Kentigern said. 'Normally you would join us in the Refectory but our meals are silent. If you follow me to the Guests' Parlour, I will bring you a tray.'

'First things first,' said Martin. I realised that this must have been Oh Dear. 'We'll fetch you some clothes. Your own were not really in a fit state to keep, I'm afraid. What we have may not be up the mark fashion-wise, but at least they will have the advantage of being'—he paused and coughed— 'clean.'

1. The opening section contained something of a disclaimer at its end. I have taken the liberty of moving it from where Columba had placed it to make a preface of it. I have placed it in italics. Even so, the style and content is so out of keeping with the rest of his memoirs that I am surprised that he did not just screw it up and bin it (as, indeed, I have been tempted to do on a number of occasions.) Yet the passage has its part to play in the discontinuous narrative that I have inherited.

A Closer Walk

The exotic surroundings—for so they seemed to me—of my shipwreck allowed much exploration both of the landscape and, later, self. At first I was puzzled: how soon could I escape the quiet and spartan world I had been dropped in? In the first days, as I puzzled on my future, other questions repeated themselves: could I recover my Kombi? Should I return to London? Where was I to travel next? Would it be possible to reconcile with Donna? Why had I behaved so badly?

My hosts seemed content to allow me to cruise along. The parts of the buildings to which I was allowed were a conundrum—on the one hand, I was permitted to wander at will, but then it would appear that access was suddenly restricted. Little signs saying 'Community Only Please' popped up on doors, gates, even one into the cemetery. There were no locks, no ropes, no substantial evidence of prohibition. It all seemed to hinge on an honesty system—we ask you not to trespass, but it is up to you. (Little did I realise that this was the CSC way: there are rules, but what you decide to do about them—and the consequences of your ignoring them—is up to you.) I was strangely compliant in this setting, despite my curiosity of what lay beyond the designated confines. Each encounter threw up the question: did I have to respect this censorship? In the end, I chose to do so. After all, these blokes had saved me—or so it seemed to me—so it would seem churlish to step over the imaginary lines in the sand they had respectfully drawn.

So I explored the places I was invited to or allowed access to. One of the first was the Guests' Parlour. This room—parlour was not a term I had encountered before—was lined with bookshelves on which sat a collection as random as I had ever seen—not that I had spent much time gazing over the spines of books. This compilation Brother Kentigern referred to as the Guests' Library. It was in the Guests' Parlour, but somehow it seemed to inhabit an independent space within it.

The Guests' Library was a mixture of novels old and new, poetry, biography, birdwatching—quite a lot of birdwatching, as it happened—historic (with a definite emphasis on the ecclesiastical) buildings. Some of which I eventually found to my tastes, though some bore exotic titles—or it seemed to me—which launched or continued to steer readers on their spiritual paths. Years later, when I was Guestmaster, oversight of these shelves was to become a part of my tasks.

The weather being very good and the countryside dotted with paths—faint tracks with stiles at either end of a field—I sought to escape the defined, but always potentially breachable, confines of the monastery. Outside there were woods, a lake, even a village some miles off into which I stumbled when lost, only to be offered friendly advice on how I might get back to my lodgings.

I started drawing up 'maps'—more scribbled instructions to myself in which I noted turns 'L' or 'R' (left or right) and invented a code somewhat at variance from the official

Ordnance Survey. CH meant church; PO accounts for the official Post Office; P was a pub; crosses and doodles designated stiles, gates and other landmarks. I realised that I had to put in some kind of legend. The code had to be understood by others. In time, I sketched out four or five walks, varying from one that took half an hour to the longest which could release someone from the monastery for three hours.

Later these peculiar hand-drawn guides to the surrounding countryside came to be approved, more or less, as official monastery issue. I would photocopy them and leave these in the Guests' Parlour. More than once a new copy would be required when a guest was caught in the rain. This, of course, was years into the future when I was acting as Guestmaster.

Guests often asked about 'good' walks. All of them were refreshing; none was too strenuous; but good exercise was gained from them. It would be pompously pious to say that somehow I found the inner walk more interesting than the outer one...

...yes, it is pompous...

The explorations of the area done, I itched for something to do. I mentioned this to Brother Kentigern. He smiled, rubbed his hand excitedly and said, 'Oh, I am sure we can find something for you. Indoors or outside?' I opted for the latter, only to be led to a vast vegetable garden.

'On your knees,' said Kentigern. He laughed when he saw the panic on my face. 'Not to pray. Weeding. Brother Garden will be here in a moment.' He left me there and soon enough Father Martin arrived, pushing the wheelbarrow that had transported me to St Candida's, gave me a hand fork and spade, a sieve to throw the weeds into, pointing out a pile to which they were destined and left me to it. For four days.

The Cloud-Filled Sky

One time, toward the end of my novitiate, I was having—as I have had, and do have still, at unregulated intervals, if I am honest—something of a spiritual crisis. Numbers in our ranks had thinned. Matthew had left, pursuing his comic graphic art. Cyril was that bit ahead of me and I thought he would make the perfect monk, as he seemed the perfect novice. But he too had quit the cloister despite his profession. Somehow, I found out much later, as his girlfriend had predicted, that the spiritual gains of foregoing female companionship— 'a waste' she had said—would not outweigh his love of her and Poplar. The first of the two won out and so he returned to Chrisp Street market. So here I was, the last of a bad lot, feeling not only drained but useless.

I sought out the Novice Master and laid it out before him. He smiled. 'Spending a lot of time in chapel?'

'Yes.'

'And reading? Both spiritual and theological?'

'Yes.'

'Mmm. Novels? Poetry?' I told him there was not a lot of time left for that sort of thing. He nodded. 'Get your jacket and your hat. Put on some boots. Meet me at the vegetable garden gate in ten minutes.' I tried to protest. The Office was in fifteen minutes. 'You leave that to me.'

I went back to my cell, threw on my jacket, stuffed my cap into a pocket and was making my way downstairs when I heard the bell for None sounding. I paused, torn between the discipline of making my way to chapel as I should have, or the choice to do as the Novice Master had advised. Here was a clash of obediences. I rushed to the boot rack, hoping (successfully as it turned out) that I would not encounter any of the brethren, slid off my sandals, took the pair of socks from the neck of one of the boots, put them and the boots on, tied up the laces and made my way like a thief to the garden gate.

The Novice Master arrived. Just before we opened the gate, he began to lead me in the Angelus. Rather than question his timing—it was not one of the appointed hours for its recitation—I gave the responses. When we had finished he said, 'I know it is the wrong time, but I assured Fr Abbot that we would pray. That will do for our Office. Now, let's go.'

He led me off on the path, through the copse of oaks some distance from the garden. The first signs of spring were evident: buds on the end of the boughs; a soft chirruping from birds as we strolled, sometimes abreast, sometimes one following the other. We walked in silence for at least twenty minutes. Every now and then the Novice Master would stop, point to a feature that may have passed me by: a rabbit scampering from the path; the nascent shoots from a bulb; a dash of colour from a bird as it flitted into or out of a tree; a strip of cloth torn from a scarf in a hedgerow. As we continued the exchange became reciprocal, not taking turns, but each of us drawing the other's attention to something of note, animate or inanimate. We made our way to a clearing atop a small hill about a mile from the House.

'Now look up.' The Novice Master's command was the first utterance made since our passing through the gate. 'Can you name them?'

There was an extensive vista of clouds. It constituted the natural equivalent of a wall map. I did my best to identify what was stretched before me. I grabbed at terms that I later learned were the life's work of Luke Howard, the 'Namer of Clouds'.

'Cumulus?'

'Big, fluffy and sparking our imagination,' came the commentary of the Novice Master. My responses followed the arc from his finger.

'Stratus.'

'Stretching across the sky like a taut rubber band.'

'Nimbus.'

'A threat of rain to come despite the sun. But not yet. We should still be dry on our return.'

'Cirrus.'

'Angels' tails. I have always wanted a painter to use a cloud like that for Gabriel.' The Novice Master's finger moved to a patch of stratus. I looked at him. 'Just to the side.'

'The moon?'

'Do you know what phase it is in?' I ran through the cycle: full, half, crescent, waxing, and plumped for waning. 'Well done,' he said. 'See how faint it is? That is not the moon's fault. There is, what? three quarters of it, ever so faintly visible, but that doesn't mean it is not all there. It's just we can't see it. Nothing wrong with the moon. There is nothing wrong with your eyes, either. It is about conditions. Normal, natural conditions that change with the movement of the earth, the moon and the planets. The orbit, the rotation, how the light from the sun is interrupted by clouds and the atmosphere. Other factors all contribute to what we can see. But the sun is still there in its entirety.'

'You brought me out here to give me a lesson in cosmology?' I said.

'Not at all, Brother. Everything we know, everything we teach—though please don't tell Father Aidan I said so—is through metaphor and analogy. The gospels are full of them. Like Jesus and Parable of the Sower.'[1]

'That always bothers me. They must have been pretty thick, the disciples. Because the explanation…well, it is little more than stating the bleeding obvious.'

'And to think Father Bartholomew wrote a whole book on that!' The Novice Master chuckled. 'The bleeding obvious. Is that what I am saying?'

It was my turn for silence. I had overstretched myself, I knew. One thing I did notice, though, was my mood had lifted. The pointlessness of monasticism was the last thing on my mind. 'I'm sorry, no.'

'All right. Cheer up,' he said. 'Now it is my turn to state the bleeding obvious. The sun is God. He is present, burning, hot, light-giving and wonderful all the time. Never stops being all those things. Yet here on earth we can miss His presence, not because He has left us, He is not there, but simply because the order of the world, our world and our part in it, can somehow hide that from us. We can't see Him. In fact, the night is a time when He gives us relief from His appearance so we can ponder in the depths of our being, in our rest, in our sleep, so we can long for His return when awake. We can glimpse His wonder in the dawn.

'All these…' He made a gesture towards the clouds, 'are

different ways of being in His presence. Some give us rain. Some take our breath away. Some amuse us. Look at that.' He pointed. 'An elephant turning into a horse made from cotton wool.' Silly as it sounded, the clouds somehow did fit the Novice Master's description.

'Another reading of the same thing: the different callings of people—lay, religious, parish priests, people going about their daily business, even people of other faiths and maybe even none. Now, for God's sake, don't tell Father Augustine. He is very big on only Christians going to heaven.'

I nodded.

'Okay, I'm stretching this a bit,' he said. 'But in for a penny, in for a pound. Try this. The clouds are the religious orders. Some tending, some active—teaching, nursing, stuff like that. Others are just playful and beautiful. Contemplatives. On one level not appearing to do very much at all. People with no reason but to ponder the brightness of God in the Son.'

'And CSC?'

'I should have seen that coming. Well we, like all the people of God, are like the moon. The Founder had a vision, if you like, of our being a satellite. We are not the earth, we do not sustain life. That's the work of the Church. We are not apart from that either. But we are caught up in this interplay of rotation, orbit and light. But any light we shine, if we are lucky enough to shine at all, is always going to be a pale reflection of that coming from a long way away, and of an intensity that we could never survive in.'

'So we are all doomed to fail?' I asked.

'Not at all. But like the phases of the moon allow an array of shapes of light because of multiple causes, clouds being only one of them, we can still show the light.'

'Let your light shine.'[2]

'Precisely,' he said. 'Now, about our pointlessness?'

I shook my head. We walked back, neither speaking nor gesturing, to the monastery where, a few months later in the chapel, I made my profession.

1. The Parable of the Sower appears in different forms in the Synoptic Gospels, Matthew 13, Mark 4 and Luke 8. They each go on to give variant explanations of the story.

2. Columba is quoting Matthew 5:16.

Two guests were waiting for the kettle to boil.

Guest One: 'Even contemplative monks pick their noses.'

A pause.

Guest Two: 'And fart. In chapel, too.'

Guest One: 'It broke my meditation. I don't think he even knew he was doing it.'

Guest Two: 'I heard one old boy let one go at the quietest part of the mass.'

Despite the snickering, these observations seemed to shock them.

I Nothing Am

My most public monastic moment was, like much of my life at St Candida's, relatively private. Friends and guests 'from the world' used to tell me of grand events—weddings, ordinations, even consecrations.

One brother, Fr Benedict, much to the opprobrium of some of the community—indeed, the few who knew the monk in question were still at odds over it years after his death— accepted the invitation to serve as a suffragan bishop. Chapter, no doubt under the influence of Fr Abbot, eventually voted to allow him to do this. The community insisted he take with him two brothers, so CSC would live as a missionary cell in the life of a diocese. There was an ongoing battle—so it was reported years later—as to who this couple of brothers should be and to whom—the Bishop or the Abbot—they were responsible. After about ten years Fr Benedict returned to Saint Candida's. Accustomed to being in authority, it is said he was peeved at not being elected Abbot. He did, however, serve as Prior to the man who was.

Some professions filled the chapel. Family, friends, colleagues from the world, would come to support, or puzzle at, the life-choice of one of their number. At these times there was always an element of tension—trying to involve those sitting in the guests' stalls, of seeking to explain the ritual, our life together, and what the neophyte's role in this would be.

No such crowd augmented the congregation when I found myself the last—and only one—of my group of novices making my vows. The others had either quit the cloister or had already made the grade. Cyril had taken this step some months before me—the Novice Master considered him cut from a better spiritual cloth. I don't think anyone at the time would have considered mine to be harder wearing.

Fr Abbot stood before me in with his pastoral staff. The Visitor, robed in a chasuble, bemitred and holding his crosier, stood at his side.

'What do you seek?' Fr Abbot said.

The Novice Master had drilled me in the responses.

'Life in Christ.'

'With whom and where do you seek to live this life?'

'By the grace of God, I would walk this path with my brethren here.'

There followed CSC's rite of admission, in which I received the belt and cross of the order and the scapular of a professed brother. Novices wore one of a lighter shade. The belt has had to be replaced a couple of times, but, by the grace of God, I still have the crucifix. After a short litany, prayers, and the joint laying on of hands by the Bishop and Fr Abbot, a blessing from the episcopal Visitor, the leader of our community gave the address, a typed copy of which he later presented to me.[1]

'The Christian life is one of celebration and sadness. Celebration because it so often presents new beginnings. Indeed, the basis of our faith is one of repeated beginnings from a particular one: the new life shown to us in the resurrection of

Jesus. And yet, there would be no resurrection if Our Lord had not truly died. And his death is rightly to be mourned. But for that he must have been truly born.

'All Christians dare to see the world in a new light. We dare to see growth in decay. We dare to see life in death. And we dare to see joy in pain.

'Every brother, no matter how long he is with us, is a gift. And for that we must thank God for His grace and thank each other for choosing to be with us, as we thank Columba today. Each is a seed that is sown in our midst. And, like the seed Jesus speaks of in the gospels, he must die so he, and we with him, can live.[2]

'Setting out on the monastic life is often portrayed in romantic terms. That is usually because those who portray it that way have never lived it.[3] Committing oneself to life in a community, one that some consider is divorced, or even a refuge, from the world, is a risk. In fact, it is a risk for all involved. Life in the cloister has its own challenges. As the sixth century abbot Columba set out on his journey with his brothers from Ireland to Iona in his coracle, so our Brother Columba is being asked to set out on a journey for which there are no reliable maps.

'Like all journeys, it will have its odd turns, its surprises and disappointments, its joys and pains. Being born again into the life of a community does not mean the troubles and anxieties of life go away. They just change. Change into new and sometimes startling forms. The quiet of the cloister[4]... the quiet of the cloister is no refuge for those who cannot get on with the world. Because the world will be right here with you.

'Jesus told his followers to carry the cross. Not his cross. Not another's cross. But each his own individual cross.[5] We ourselves are the greatest cross we have to bear. We carry our cross, our selves, individually and, in the community we commit ourselves to, we carry it together. Brother Columba, Barry, welcome to this cross. And welcome from those who will seek to share its load with you.'

Father Abbot turned to the brethren. 'Brothers, I ask you to pray for Columba. He has been tested on the way. And the testing will continue. As it continues for us all every day. Thanks be to God, without whom we should always be found lacking. Amen.'

The service continued with holy communion. And so I found myself committed to a quiet collection of men who took to the routine of life, punctuated by bells, prayer and work. And each other. It was where I thought I would spend all my days.

After the service there was a party, with wine and cake. Fr Abbot was right. We did not know where the journey would take us. I never imagined Bethnal Green or Care Home as part of it. Or how it would end. And, by the grace of God, I still don't.

1. I found a copy of the address from Columba's profession among the papers in the envelope he had left for me. I have taken a liberty by inserting here to assist his narrative.

2. The Abbot was recalling John 12:24— 'Very truly, I tell you, unless a grain of wheat falls into the earth and dies, it remains just a single grain; but if it dies, it bears much fruit.'

3. 'This got a titter from the choir stalls', Columba had annotated in the margin.

4. 'Another laugh from the choir stalls', according to Columba's marginal notes.

5. Matthew 10:38— '… whoever does not take up the cross and follow me is not worthy of me.'

Today in chapel we sang, 'One Church, One Faith, One Lord.' If only.

A Row of Books

Books are essential to, if not the stuff of, a monastery. We were a far way from the Scriptorium, though some of us (like Matthew) could have been stars in the firmament of illustrated manuscripts. His wit would have enlivened many a dull chapter detailing the slaughter, conquests, rapes and seizing of property that make up the Histories in the Old Testament.

I had, probably unfairly, a reputation for being a non-reader at school and beyond. But such a calling was impossible at St Candida's. I read voraciously but it has to be admitted that my sustenance was not of the academic bent. Even in the Novitiate I found much of the set texts of intellectual stuff on the Christian faith more impenetrable than edifying. It was gratifying to hear one novice, fresh from his studies in Oxford, telling the Novice Master that Systematics was 'at worst failed, at best second rate, philosophy.' Matthew captured the NM's reaction perfectly in a cartoon that was lost as quickly as it appeared.

I suppose my sustenance was secondary. Of course, our days are drenched in the Bible: the Offices, the mass, private and public reading. But it was to 'the lesser literature', as Fr Aidan once called it (with the odd exception) that I took recourse to. Simpler spirituality—Thérèse of Lisieux, the easier bits of Julian of Norwich and, to Father Abbot's surprise, *The Book of Privy Counsel*. And biographies of saints and leading lights of the church. Some were couched in difficult prose. These were cast aside for those of a more popular appeal. Why should the life of an interesting man or woman be made dull by turgid writing? A few of these were particularly entertaining, even ridiculous. How a personality like Christina the Astonishing was tolerated, let alone venerated, is beyond me.[1]

And novels. (I wonder if this was my mother's influence coming out? All those stories she wrote for the Women's Weekly.) I found so much more to understand about the world through fiction than I did from many of the works recommended by the Novice Master. Though we found common ground in C. S. Lewis. Him I could read all day. Especially the Aslan books. It was probably for that that I was never apportioned the duty of community Librarian.

It did fall to me, however, during my time as Guestmaster, to oversee the Guesthouse library. This expanded as many retreatants would often leave a novel they had brought with them. These ranged from the high- to the low-brow. I expected to manage something like a book exchange, but we gained more than we lost by the exercise. Some of the books, it has to be admitted, were a bit 'out there'. Every now and then one would have to be binned or go into the recycling. I didn't think it was the kind of thing we should have on our shelves. I sometimes made this decision only after I had read it.

Some retreatants would seek religion in and through fiction—novels about saints, sagas looking at a religious order through different decades of the twentieth century, ethical dilemmas worked out in imaginary (or thinly disguised autobiographical) settings. I read—and read them still—again and again. There was a particularly rich seam from the mine of murder mysteries, from the pulp to the well crafted, set in monasteries and convents, usually with a professed member of the community acting as the equivalent of the DCI.

Care Home has a similar set of shelves. There is always an alarming number of non-returned items from the local library—I wonder if St Peter at the Pearly Gates presents borrowers with a statement of overdue fines?—which sit among books that I initially found startling. But, as I came to reflect, why should the reading of a range of adults, one of whom is the former brilliant academic I know as Father Abbot, who share a residence only by virtue of need of oversight or care, be restricted to pap? There was precious little romantic fiction to be found on the shelves after my first foray. I happily scour this treasure trove from the classical to the contemporary.

What I miss is the quiet that I so long associated with reading. The incessant cacophony of music, competing radio stations and blaring televisions, the raised voices of residents, staff and visitors, makes it difficult to read here. Sometimes the volume is no more than the result of the hard of hearing mistakenly thinking they have not been heard. The lounge can be a refuge, but not for long. Sooner or later a bewildered or confused resident will come in and break the peace, and with it my concentration. And then there is Fr Aidan. He is my brother and it is my duty to sit with him. Every now and then I read aloud to him. But his awareness rightly challenges me: who are these people? What is going on? What have they to do with him?

Better, then, to read from the Bible. I tend to keep to the Gospels. Even such a small repertoire is inexhaustible. After all, that is all the Church has of the life of the Saviour. The Word made flesh is literature enough.

1. Various accounts of this Belgian saint are both alarming and amusing as, in routine prayer or elevated from her coffin at her funeral rites, Christina hovers over her sisters in chapel, so offended was she by the odour of their sins.

EDITOR'S NOTE

What follows were all on separate pieces of papers. I assume they were written at different times, but the theme of decline— 'change and decay in all around I see'—militates for their being brought together. Clearly this theme is reflective of many people's concerns about loss of physical and mental capacities. There is something almost touching in the way that the community, and its buildings are part of the journey to ashes and dust.

Old Chapel

It was not only within the cloister that signals of change were evident. There seemed to be reminders of the road travelled by those outside our community when they visited the monastery.

Some signals were clearly to be seen in our regulars, men and women who came each year to spend time with us—no, that is not right; they came to spend time with God in our company, as Fr Aidan would have reminded me. These people, around whom we built a routine into which they could float in and out—no, wrong again; people were admitted to the rhythm of the house to gain some connection to a pattern lost outside our walls. These people also sustained us, bringing in concerns from outside our experience. It was a gift to watch them—some of them at least—relax, unwind and find a deeper sense of peace that, by the grace of God, we somehow were able to offer to others. But, like us, they became increasingly frail and fragile.

Some of our guests, clergy and lay, would begin to slow down, resiling from the long, bracing walks that so re-energised them in years past, to long stretches in a comfortable chair in the Guests' parlour. Many would look out the window, as if searching for some divine message in the gardens or the rolling hills beyond them. The sky and hovering birds drew their attention for prolonged periods, the viewer relishing in sights that normally would pass unnoticed.

Sleep is no stranger to the retreatant, however experienced. Nor is there any shame attached to it. Indeed, well before I served as Guestmaster, I had witnessed the exhausted faces on those coming into the Guest Wing. The first day or so they would be confined to their cells. I initially assumed them to hard at prayer. 'No,' said Brother Bernard, 'they'll be in no state for that yet. Listen as you walk. You will hear them laying down the burden of daily life. After they have done that, if they are lucky, they may get a minute or two of the blissful joy of the silent prayer Teresa of Avila writes about.' Indeed, he was right. The Guest Wing would reverberate with snoring.

Guests would return, slouching, shuffling, until, announced or not, they made their last visit to St Candida's. The hair would thin, grey, become less groomed. The clothes harked back to an earlier fashion, tweeds autumning into the utility brand of the elderly—the elasticated waists, the stained jackets, the velcroed, rather than laced, shoes. Some would add their shuffle to those of the more fragile brethren on the way into chapel. Like their professed brothers in the stalls, they would sometime lose their place in the ever-turning pages of the Office Book. They found stairs a similar challenge to some on the other side of the enclosure. Competition broke out for booking the ground floor guest room which, as had happened for the monks, was a concession to fragility.

Occasionally we would get a card or a letter from someone who knew them, telling us of their deaths, requesting that a mass be offered for the repose of their souls. But it was mostly silence.

And it was the silence they came for. At first. As the old timers thinned our younger, newer retreatants became more demanding. We were often unable to respond to what they presented as requests (which were entirely reasonable to them). Fr Abbot refused to get a computer for the house. He saw it as yet another development in distraction. He might as well have said work of the devil.

The mobile phone reception was non-existent at first, then compromised, but always poor. Likewise we seemed to have been placed in one part of Dorset that was never going to get superfast anything, let alone broadband. Indeed, for many of us, that was the attraction. But the Guestmaster would be made to realise that not all people come to a place of prayer and silence for what we think is attractive and essential. Why did we not have wi-fi? Why did we not agitate for a booster to improve our facilities? How could we exist in such a communications black hole? The questions became increasingly technical and the questioners concomitantly aggressive. Somehow we were no longer a retreat from the world, we were despite it.

More vibrant centres of Christian hospitality rivalled us: screens, bands, eruptions of joy and intentionally missional, as one retreatant told me. (I have no idea what he meant.) Occasionally some of their patrons would come to us, having heard of the counter-culture we embodied. Some, as refugees from the new centres, came for the silence, routine, the dull drudgery of discipline the monastery had to offer. Others reacted to what we were and did. Or did not do. For them the style and expression of their faith paraded under a number of words—Spirit-filled, charismatic, exciting. This, one told me, was what made such places 'relevant'. One of the brothers, no doubt, would have quipped, 'Relevant to what?', before giving a lecture on how it could not stand on its own. I didn't have to ask. It was pretty clear. It was relevant to him, and the world he moved in. We were not. A one-time retreatant, who left after a day and a half, less than halfway through his projected, booked and paid for stay, considered us irredeemably lax and liberal. He described himself as Bible-believing.

Our next abbot set out to bend the community to our visitors' needs and requests. Or were they demands? His winning argument was based on Christian service—we were hosting people whose needs had to be met as guests. He cited the epistle of James, chapter 2, saying the community was meeting the bodily needs of our guests. Some of the brethren tried to counter, unsuccessfully, that catering for modern communications was hardly an essential of charity. Vigorous, theological and social, debate followed on the nature— essential or otherwise—of God's grace and charity.

The abbot won the day and this led, as it always did, to an invasion of builders, and a disruption of our established pattern of prayer and work. When it was finished the abbot urged us to be open and allow a settling in period. For some of the brothers, it ushered a sense of ongoing unsettledness.

Chapter became the venue for vexed questions. Was an email sent by computer in the evening a breaking of Greater Silence? For some it was clearly a breach. One should not be working anyway. For others it encapsulated the problem: was being a contemplative finding stillness in a world which changed no matter our rhythm or response? Older brothers would recount earlier disputes—electricity in the chapel; central heating throughout the house; the internal phone system; the alteration to the pattern of Offices to keep abreast in changes of language and the Church of England's liturgies;

the restoration of a house style by one abbot; the musical regimes set, maintained, changed and abandoned.

All of this was part of our daily life as our numbers fell. One brother, straight from Cambridge, completed his doctorate while a Novice. This caused consternation among some of the brethren but Aidan, who was Novice Master, was in favour. Some brothers grumbled—there are grumblers in every community—arguing that the research took the novice 'away from his vocation'. It was a serious distraction, they said, from his formation in the monastic life. Having an academic—and an active one at that—for his overseer in monastic formation did his cause no harm.

I don't know who could be judged right in this. The brother, unlike Fr Aidan, later left us to take up an academic post, produced a long list of books, then got a pointy hat. He made a series of retreats with us some years back. It was not a happy experience for him or us. It served to remind some that the grumblers had been right—he would never stick. He was more interested in other things than silent contemplation.

He would spend quite a bit of time with Aidan who was similarly academic, but seemed to carry it off in a different manner. As Aidan's stature decreased—perhaps the bishop had noticed the falling off of his acuity—so did the visits. He recently wrote a well received memoir, which contained long reminiscences of his short time in the cloister.

A guest to the Guestmaster: 'What do you do for fun?'

There was a long pause.

Fr William replied, 'I think we strive for contentment. It is a bit of a struggle, but fun enough.'

Wash Me Throughly–1

This morning was change of bed linen day. For a few of us that is a weekly occurrence. For others it is daily. When it gets to the situation when it is more than twice a day a case conference is held to decide what is the best care plan for the individual. To that end, getting residents mobile and clad in incontinence wear is to the benefit of all. It contains the problem.

I usually strip my bed, take my sheets and pillow case to the worker pushing the trolley. With me, at least, it is something less burdensome than others. I like to maintain my own room, much as I did my own cell. I am usually rewarded with a clean set of bed linen—usually the stripping of the bed and its replacement is done in stages, if not by different carers—but most of the domestic workers know that I will be ready to put my room in order. I do that, having turned my mattress in anticipation, and make up the bed for the week ahead.

This routine has been a strangely comforting one for me. As part of my duties as Guestmaster, I used to maintain the accommodation of those who stayed with us but CSC, as did many retreat houses, relied on guests to change their sheets prior to departure. This got easier with the adoption of fitted sheets and the use of continental duvets rather than blankets.

But even then, it did seem beyond the capacity of some guests, usually married men, I am both ashamed and surprised to note. (Monks are trained and expected to be relatively self-reliant in this regard).

One bishop, who had a reputation for pomposity, subverted all expectations during his first and only stay at St Candida's by being a truly humble co-resident. He insisted that he be called by his Christian name, not even Father before it, which perturbed some of the brethren. His maintenance of silence for his retreat allowed all to avoid any discomfort. His vesture was anything but prelatial—not a dog collar to be seen. Certainly he never appeared in a cassock, purple or otherwise. He not only changed his linen before departure but, on his own insistence, had turned the mattress before he did so, vacuumed the room, including bottoming out (as I learned they call it in the East End), and scrubbed the sink.

'It rather puts me out of a job,' I quipped when he asked for the hoover.

'Don't mind that, Brother,' he said. 'I am sure you will find plenty else to do.'

The routines of clearing and cleaning rooms was one I looked on with quiet satisfaction. Having read of the horror stories of some bed and breakfast operators in a Sunday paper, I realise that even our most untidy and troublesome guests were relatively easy work. The BandB owners' accounts of broken furniture and fixtures, towels used as toilet paper, blood and other bodily fluids seemingly sprayed in all directions, made the retreatant a focussed and pliable client.

There were some things you came to expect: clipped toe- and finger-nails. What was it that made a retreat the venue for such activity? Cast off packaging and various used personal hygiene products—dental floss, razor blades, cotton buds—as well as stationery, read or abandoned books, notepads. Then there were the forgotten trappings of modern life that needed returning—the phone charger, on occasion a phone itself, the cord for the laptop or other device. We kept a store of recycled padded envelopes for their despatch, trips to the post office being one of the Guestmaster's duties. These were really minor irritants. Though, in my less charitable moments, they could became Everests of resentment.

For all that, it did seem that slipping a fitted sheet onto a mattress, with a straight, neat mattress protector beneath, was beyond the skill set of some. It would be in seeking to correct these shortcomings I would detect the occasional evidence of sexual self-satisfaction. Even clergy take things in hand from time to time.

I loved the completion of tasks. Clearing up, putting the washing on, hanging it out to dry in the sun when the weather allowed, or in the long drying room by the Guest Wing boiler, the subsequent folding and stacking in the linen press—all that was part of the Founder's original vision, was a prayerful, calming ritual. All such work somehow gave me a fulfilment. In my elevated moments—and these were rare—I imagined myself a sort of Brother Lawrence, exercising his ministry of minutiae, and in doing so immersing myself in my practice of the presence of God.[2] But I am far from being such a mystic. Lawrence's gift was to channel his thoughts to God. One of the great English contemplatives, Mother Maribel of Wantage, is quoted to have advised a novice having trouble with prayer, 'Don't try to do things. All you have to do is to provide a channel sufficiently clear of rubbish for God to work through. It is his love coming through you, his light shining through you that matters. Our poor little efforts are nothing. It is all so simple, and like all simple things so hard to do.'[3] Needless to say, there was plenty in Columba's channels that needed dredging.

Here in Care Home such satisfaction was temporary. Getting my cell—no, my room—in order was provisional. There was little chance to go to it and receive instruction[4], as my vocation now was one of accompaniment to Father Abbot. To be with him meant to leave my space for the common one that was also his. On a good day we could do the office together, attend the weekly mass in one of the sitting rooms, even go for a stroll around the home's garden. But mostly it was making myself visible, my habit and scapular somehow supplying the reassurance a fretful, forgetful priest required.

My duties have become focussed on a person, rather than on than on what some call creature comforts. Or the menial tasks of life. Of course, it has always been a mixture of the two but, as I hand my dirty sheets to the Care Home worker, and receive their replacements, as I did today, I thank God for the little things that allow me to help others help myself.

1. Once again Columba has resorted to the Book of Common Prayer 1662. This rendering of verse 2 of Psalm 51, leaves out an 'o', in 'throughly'. Despite that, many people use the more modern word 'thoroughly' when reading it on sight.

2. Brother Lawrence of the Resurrection, to give him his full name in religion, was a 17th-century lay brother in a Carmelite monastery in Paris. His tasks were mainly in the kitchen. Despite this, his sayings and wisdom have come to be regarded as classics, captured in a book *The Practice of the Presence of God*.

THE REST IS SILENCE

3. This is quoted in the biography by Sister Janet C.S.M.V. *Mother Maribel of Wantage*, SPCK, London, 1973, p 34.

4. This is a version of an oft-quoted aphorism attributed to many spiritual teachers, St Benedict among them. One of the best known renderings of the advice ends with the claim that the cell contains in itself everything requisite for instruction.

Come into the Parlour, Maud[1]

I don't think I had ever heard anyone speak of a parlour until I arrived at St Candida's. The very word conjured up for me special spaces, perhaps those 'good' rooms into which great-aunts were posted to sit and chat with my parents, children not to be admitted into such polite company.

A similar thing occurred with nuns, so I learned from my Roman Catholic friends, so they could eat cake and drink afternoon tea away from prying eyes—children's or relatives'. Why they demanded this, or people conceded to it, is beyond me. I have been told that nuns hunted in pairs—they were not allowed to be out alone, even with their immediate family— and until certain reforms within the Roman discipline, only a fellow sister was allowed to see the crumbs fall to what was by repute the best china.

My ears should have pricked up at the mention of a parlour when I was first ushered into one after my rescue in the wheelbarrow. But such was my addled brain that I hardly registered the dropping of this strange term. Brother Kentigern brought me a tray to the thus designated room for my first solitary repast at CSC. Perhaps I had brought my contagion with me? One that could not be risked in the Refectory of professed brothers?

Having never heard of such places, they began to proliferate. The Abbot had a parlour. The Prior had one named after or for him, but it was used as a space between the guests' area and the enclosure. Small groups of retreatants, priests or ordinands discerning possible vocations to the monastic life, would gather in the Prior's Parlour. It was also a place where spiritual direction—routine, one-off or emergency—was offered. It was part of the monastery, but still outside the perimeters of the professed. (There was also a room/confessional off the guests' section of the chapel.)

The Guests' Parlour was, at the time of my arrival, a place of communal recreation. The walls were lined with books. It was stocked with comfortable chairs, often with wings to support a nodding neck, in a circle approximating a potential view of the fireplace in which, in the latter part of autumn and winter, logs may be set ablaze. Over the years central heating was relied on to provide protection from the chill, so the company of other silent readers was abandoned, a development welcomed in part by the Guestmaster, among whose tasks was the clearing and cleaning of the fireplace. With no fire to gaze into, people tended to remain in their rooms or took to the chapel. It seemed, or so said Brother Librarian, people had lost the ability to sit with others in company in individual pursuits. He used the term 'to recreate in silence in company'. But then he was from another era. Guests either needed to socialise—talk or interact—or to be completely on their own. The search for solitude overtook the desire for communal silence. Though, while walking along the corridors of the Guest Wing, you could hear the not always muted sounds of radios and one side of conversations on mobile phones. As Guestmaster I found myself the sometimes unwilling interventionist in having to promote the idea of our collective commitment to quiet.

The Guests' Parlour also housed a library. The nature of the literature there ran the range from the pious, through the pompous to the populist. The simple summation was this: it takes all kinds.[2]

Such parallels were not immediate at Care Home, particularly given that I have arrived at a latter part of its evolution. I suppose that, like a monastery, there had originally been one television around which all residents would gather to receive news or entertainment in common. I imagine the inevitable disagreements about who wants to watch what when would spark, simmer and sometimes erupt. To avoid controversies, different parlours in different wings of the home were given over to different stations. But if someone had been wheeled and abandoned in the wrong room, who could correct the oversight? Then, of course, most residents were not liable to the television licence, so proliferation was inevitable. Indeed, when I insisted that no such provision be made in my room—Fr Aidan's was a different issue—I was looked on with a mixture of bewilderment and alarm. It was beyond the experience of the manager.

From time to time I attempted to recreate monastic recreation in Care Home. But it was never a success. Sitting with a book, or in quiet companionship with Father Aidan, if he was capable of it, I would relish the relative quiet. There was always a buzz of television, the room alarms, shouts or other sounds to ensure silence was never allowed to establish itself. This was also a lure. Some of the wandering confused would see us together and seek help, reassurance or direction—sometimes all three—as they found themselves adrift in the constrained freedom of the home. Or those clear of mind would come in looking for company with someone of a common state, someone with whom conversation was possible. But finding contemporary common substance was difficult. Often talk would be led by the past—nostalgia, memories, recollections, reminiscences—so that apart from the latest news items or sports events, or more likely the weather, the now was abandoned.

The pattern witnessed at CSC was repeated—at least within and by me—of moving from the social to the solitary. The parlour was a place of distraction. Sometimes I would seek to experience the larger space. But Fr Abbot was often uncomfortable in such a setting, unless a religious service was being conducted. For him, I suppose, this was not a parlour, but the chapel. A place where the community, such as it was, experienced some collective spiritual solace. But even during the weekly mass he would sometimes drift off to sleep, or be entranced by another resident's sleeping, clothing, posture. Or he would look out the window with concentration on events outside our confines. This, ironically, only heightened a sense of imprisonment in me.

In the monastery, at least in the Abbot's, Prior's, Novices', Guests' parlours were places that blurred work and refreshment. What we have here are offices—places of administration rather than those of prayer. They are where the manager, the administrator, the Care Co-ordinator are to be found. Parlours have vanished, another casualty of a world set on keeping up to date, however illusory or ephemeral that may be.

1. Columba is making a play on the words of Alfred Lord Tennyson *Come*

Into The Garden, Maud, and the subsequent song, with music by Michael William Balfe.

2. Columba has written more fully about the Guests' library, and literature in the life of the monastery, in *A Row of Books*, *Spines Displayed* and tangentially in *A Closer Walk*.

Spines Displayed

Books in the monastery library, such was the view aired a few times at Chapter, should be more than a reflection of the interests of Brother Librarian. That may have been the view of those of us not schooled, as of some of the brethren were, in academic theology.

The Novice Master warned us quite early in our novitiate. 'Brothers, never fall into the trap of saying you are not theologians. It is true that among our number here are some big thinkers, men who could happily take their place at a college high table. But they have chosen—or have they been chosen? —to take on our common life as their burden. Whatever you do—study, pray, clean, cook, work in the garden—whatever you do is done in the presence of and with thought of God. That is theology. Every monk, every Christian, is a theologian.'

For all that, most of the library's books seemed to be there for my dusting rather than reading. It was a cornucopia of knowledge and I noticed that most members of the community, new and old, sought the classics—writings of the Desert Fathers, the mystics, the simple saints—over the latest considerations or controversies from the universities.

Yet we had new books regularly. There were the works of

Fr Aidan, which some brothers adopted as required reading. Fr Cuthbert, who for a while became something of a star in popular religious literature, had several on the shelves. This was just before the major papers abandoned reviewing books of a religious nature.[1] His timing was with the zeitgeist: a breadth of experience, encounters with Eastern mysticism—mainly Zen Buddhism, but some from India—that had an enthusiast's vigour and a natural educator's clarity. Cuthbert was repeatedly asked to speak at events and conferences, both church-based and secular—and even appeared on television a few times. These appearances proved popular. Here was a 'with it' monk in a habit.

He churned out (that is possibly a needlessly derisory classification of his working methods) a number of books that had three effects. One was more touring given over to reading, speaking and conference engagements. The second was a significant contribution to CSC's income through royalties. The third was a mixed blessing—an influx of people expecting to find a monk along the lines of Maharishi Mahesh Yogi, only to be disappointed when they encountered a member of a traditional western monastic house. Cuthbert struggled to get people who had read his books to understand that his movement was an inner one, of how to adapt within the tradition of the Church, rather than aping Eastern mores.

There was some grumbling among the ranks and it was thought Fr Cuthbert had become somewhat big-headed. It was said—gossip is poisonous in the cloister, try as we do to avoid it—that Fr Abbot had called him in and threatened to curtail his engagements if he did not walk a little more humbly. Whether it was the result of this rumoured encounter, or that some other cleric was found to be the next media darling, Fr

Cuthbert seemed a little subdued as a consequence.

Some years later he was seconded to a theological college where his brief was Prayer and Spirituality. He oversaw a raft of ordinands and priests who were exposed to, if not skilled in, meditation as a practice to support ministry.

'I thought,' said one wag, 'that was the lot of every cleric.'

Cuthbert returned to us, spent a number of years writing a large tome which sought to collate, distil and popularise his thought. So many things, though, had moved on. His publishers, hoping his earlier popularity would outweigh the negative reviews of the hardback mainly in the Church press—only one broadsheet gave space to a lukewarm assessment—gave it prominence but it failed to draw the kind of sales his earlier, more popular paperbacks had.

Some even thought that this would lead to Fr Cuthbert's quitting Saint Candida's. It did not. The whole enterprise appeared to settle him. Once he told me, 'Well, acceptance and resignation is the lot of a monk, whatever the ups and downs,' and Fr Abbot made him Guestmaster. He enjoyed the work. It was something of a surprise when he started to complain of aches and pains—monks are discouraged from making their own organ recital the subject of conversation—which were the overture to a short, but particularly torturous, illness when cancer was detected in various parts of his anatomy. Such were the complexities of his treatment, and our inability to cope with it—despite having a medical doctor at that time serving as Infirmarian—Fr Abbot reluctantly sent Fr Cuthbert first to a hospital and, at the end, to a hospice.

Which has taken me a long way from the books at Care Home. That was the stimulus to my sitting down and taking up my pen. The shelves in what would have been called the

Guests' Library have been a great source of meditative activity for me. (We would have simply called it work at CSC.)

After a discussion with the Activities Co-ordinator (please, not another singalong of war-time songs—most of us here now are too young to remember) I was given permission to oversee the collection. There were some great conundra. The first was the number of unreturned local library books. Despite being clearly marked as such, and lacking the formerly used slips of paper that had the borrowing history on them, you could always tell how overdue a book was. I guessed these dated from the time when the mobile library would call. This service had been phased out some time before Fr Aidan and I arrived.

I questioned the Activities Co-ordinator a number of times about the matter but it became apparent the only resolution to the situation was the one I adopted. I collected all the library books, put them in a shopping trolley and set out to the library by Bethnal Green tube. The desk clerk displayed a mixture of surprise, annoyance and aggravation. Some books were no longer on the database; others had been 'withdrawn from circulation'; and one or two were welcomed as a return of something rare.

A similar mixture of emotions came over me in the following weeks and months as other errant stock somehow came to rest on the shelves to which I had sought to put in order. I did this by establishing three sections: Fiction, Non-Fiction and Large. There was another set of shelves in the area by the lift. These took what I considered my rejects—a vast collection of Mills and Boon and other Romantica—which bubbled up like a mysterious water source after I had begun work.

The library was not catalogued, though I became well acquainted with its contents and any disturbances to them. Alphabetically aligned within the three sections, the stock displayed a startling breadth of interest from highbrow literary fiction, rare editions of classics, to obscurities from all manner of authors. It was a testament, if one were needed, to the amazing dormancy of faded memory of the home's residents.

Those residents—the clichéd little old ladies and dotty old men to some—had delved into the vast complexity of human thought and imagination. Collected short stories of Vladimir Nabokov, obscure New Zealand poetry, arcane scientific musings, history, sociology, philosophy, along with numbers of texts more popular and predictable. I felt a humbling pride, as I used to at the monastery, to be among people whose gifts were either ignored or camouflaged in their residential environment. I only wish I had not acquiesced to the Trustees' advice to leave all of Fr Aidan's oeuvre behind.

'But don't you see, Brother,' the Chair had said, 'to take any or all of the works creates a problem of selection. Best to follow my earlier advice. Set forth with vigour and confidence. Think of it as taking only the one tunic!'[2]

So I left with Fr Aidan, like Lot and his family, fighting the urge not to succumb to the temptation to look back and, like his wife, become a pillar of salt.[3]

1. I think Columba is referring to works of an explicit Christian nature rather than religion in general.

2. An oblique reference to Luke 9:3 and the other synoptic gospels.

3. Genesis 19:26

Wash Me Throughly—2

I enjoyed being a Guestmaster for its routines: the welcoming, the orientation walk or, if I recognised a returnee, bringing them up to speed with changes in architecture or practice of the House. Some were inevitably interested in the membership of the community—comings and goings since their last visit. I liked marshalling them into chapel for the first time, and showing what followed what in the Offices.

Most guests looked after themselves. Some clergy were so easy the Guestmaster was almost redundant. They attended what they wanted. They slept. They made their way into and out of Refectory and Chapel and followed the unspoken rules of both. They brought a book to read or could be found browsing in the Guests' Library. They would embody the maxim of the retreat having two compass points of retreat—to and from. What those were was brought with them.

Some came for spiritual direction, to renew their acquaintance with a priest or brother. (I never sought to act in this capacity.) A few came for academic supervision, especially when Fr Aidan was still sought after by some universities.

Many came exhausted. Many left refreshed. Some came burdened and left, if not lightened, resolved to find a way to ease the load they bore. None, as far as I know, were broken. Crashes tended to happen elsewhere.

A common request, at least in the early days, was for a priest to hear a confession. Some needed this almost on arrival, as though rest and recuperation were impossible without it, while others used the time to sleep, walk, to reflect before they felt ready to be shriven.

My task was to get the right fit with little or no information about the penitent and the priest to listen to a Confession. Some would have formed a habit of seeing one priest in particular and request a session with him. For others, it was up to me. Fortunately, as I have learned myself over the years, most priests are more than ready to exercise this aspect of their ministry. It is, as Fr Augustine once told me, where the essence of priestly vocation is exercised outside the mass.

That is not to say it always went smoothly. Only once did the dissatisfaction of the sacramental encounter ever splash back on me. The retreatant, a layman in a demanding City job, came from the chapel muttering. I looked at him.

'You could have warned me that he was an unforgiving sod.'

I was truly surprised. I had arranged for him to see the monk to whom I made my own confession, a man I had always found open-hearted, generous and, some might say, something of a soft touch. But not in this instance. Life in a monastery has a certain rhythm and the sin of a monk is often one that merely disturbs the pattern of life. And those in the world perhaps want to be let off the hook for doing what they do. Or just being who they are. I can't really say in the case of the guest. What happened, apart from his comment, is still kept within the confines of the sacramental seal.

On other occasions the relief was palpable. The atmosphere of the Guest Wing would lift as someone emerged from the grey wash of disappointment to a climate of clear air. Being the midwife to such a holy encounter was a wonder.

We were reciting Psalm 40 at the Office. We got to verse 13[1] and I spotted Fr Augustine's bald head in front of me. It was all I could do not to laugh. Fr Abbot would certainly not have been amused.

1. For innumerable troubles have come about me;
my sins have overtaken me so that I cannot look up;
they are more in number than the hairs of my head,
and my heart fails me.—from the *Common Worship* Psalter.

The Day the Music Died

It was an acknowledgement that things had already fallen apart, rather than herald that they were about to, when Fr Abbot ruled in Chapter one morning that singing in Choir was to be halted.

Dwindling numbers and age had compromised the once famed sound from the stalls. A number of brothers had been singers: in church choirs, choral scholars at university, a couple had even earned their living in the world by their voices—one as a member of the chorus of the Royal Opera House (though he had more trouble blending than most of us, even the untutored, by virtue of the power of his gift)—and the capacity of these acted as an incentive to those of us not so vocally blessed.

Performance of, and the attendant rehearsals for, chanting and singing formed a significant part of our life together. The routine preparation for chanting of the Offices would be held in the place of their recitation, the choir stalls. Brother Music would ensure we knew what was down to be sung in the week ahead and any slippage that had been noted in the past seven days would be corrected with humour or admonishment. Preparation, maintenance and repair were the watchwords in chapel as much as anywhere else in the monastery.

Many guests said they came on retreat at St Candida's because of the singing. One told me during my time as Guestmaster, 'It is how I always imagined prayer should sound. The monks make the noise I hear in my head when I pray alone.' Fr Abbot had once even turned down the offer of a commercial recording of some of our Offices. Such ventures, he said, disrupted the rhythm and nature of community.

The glory of timbre, the listening to each other, the blending of voices, the subtlety of cadences, enhanced by the chapel's acoustic—all were fractured as the numbers diminished and the voices cracked and creaked. It was no-one's fault, Fr Abbot assured us; it was just part of life. He pointed out, perhaps wisely but certainly not diplomatically, to the book of Ecclesiastes:

Remember your creator in the days of your youth, before the days of trouble come, and the years draw near when you will say, 'I have no pleasure in them'; before the sun and the light and the moon and the stars are darkened and the clouds return with the rain; on the day when the guards of the house tremble, and the strong men are bent, and the women who grind cease working because they are few, and those who look through the windows see dimly; when the doors on the street are shut, and the sound of the grinding is low, and one rises up at the sound of a bird, and all the daughters of song are brought low; when one is afraid of heights, and terrors are in the road; the almond tree blossoms, the grasshopper drags itself along and desire fails; because all must go to their eternal home, and the mourners will go about the streets; before the silver cord is snapped, and the golden bowl is broken, and the pitcher is broken at the fountain, and the wheel broken at the cistern, and the dust returns to the earth as it was, and the breath returns to God who gave it. Vanity of vanities, says the Teacher; all is vanity.[1]

It was, for some, more evidence that things would never return to the glory days. Sensing the disquiet, Fr Abbot said, 'I don't want to invoke the rule of obedience. That is not my way. But it is part of my office to give oversight, not for ruling, but to reflect reality of life in our community. Brothers, we need to see that this change is inevitable. To hanker for what is lost is not to see the moment of now. It is nostalgia. Wonderful as it was, it can be no longer. It is certainly no fault of Brother Music. Or, indeed, of ourselves. So we must look ahead. For some it means taking up new things, adapting to new technologies. For me, change is an acceptance. We are greyer. We are more stooped. And we are fewer. Change is upon us in the bodies and the body of our community. It is wise to embrace it. We will now need to be attentive, maybe even for the first time, to the discipline of speaking all our prayers.'

Grumbling continued for a while. Predictably—or should I have written ironically?—the voices of discontent were loudest from those from whom the bloom of vocal tone had most noticeably deserted. When they accepted Fr Abbot's instruction, as we were bound to do, the offices began to assume a gentler, coherent phase. But it, too, seemed like a living an Agatha Christie novel as, one by one, we found our ranks reducing in number even further.

When Fr Aidan could no longer manage the various Office books the lot fell to me. Singing a song in a strange land is hard enough. In this old people's home it is a challenge. Saying it alone can be a torture.

1. Ecclesiastes 12. 1-9

May the God of hope fill you with all joy and peace in believing, so that you may abound in hope by the power of the Holy Spirit.[1]

1. Romans 5:13

Support Us
All The Day Long

Reminders of the fragility of the community could be seen in furniture. It started in the bathrooms: rails by the baths, the corral around the loos. It then crept into public spaces: the doubling of the railings to the stairs; the filling in of gaps on the landings so that no arm would go unsupported.

Chapter one morning was given over to an extraordinary discussion. Would the Order install a lift, or would some of those who currently had cells in the upper dormitory migrate to the ground floor? The latter won the day, but not without opposition. Some of the community had been in their cells for decades. Why should fragility move them out? Then there were the incontrovertible but pointless points—no such action used to be required; we lived as brothers in all things, even frailty.

Commonsense won out and so a long, invasive building programme eventuated in the provision of four ground floor cells. The community lost a parlour that had been effectively a reading room near, but separate from, the library.

Indications of the loss of physical powers even spread to the chapel. Some prayer stools and mats were first replaced by hard chairs, then armchairs and later by open spaces to allow wheelchairs to be drawn up in front of the Blessed Sacrament.

Other signals were on and in us: some brothers began to sway as they walked, a premonitory posture that a hip or knee replacement would be required; hair turned grey, thinned or vanished; lines appeared on faces; lenses of glasses thickened. Younger or fitter brothers were routinely recruited to push wheelchairs or accompany their elders to hospital appointments. The visit of the local GP to became longer and more complicated.

All this became more apparent as younger men came in decreasing numbers to test their vocation—a test we increasingly appeared to fail. Some lasted as long as the end of the novitiate. Two even made their profession. But something in them, or us, or the mere chemistry of being a modern monastic failed to gel. For a while we had a series of older men, often after retirement or retrenchment from their worldly professions, who came to live among us. A few of them stuck, but not many. The change of lifestyle was too jarring. For all this, I somehow became the youngest member of the community. But I, too, was getting older.

Indications of decay were also evident in our cells. The bed, the table, the chair—there was not much to augment. But the time came for some monks when their sleeping accommodation had to be more adaptable. They had difficulties in getting in and out of bed. Clothing, baths, transport became a community issue. Chapter meetings were often given over to consideration of how we could integrate the failing powers of some members into the life of monastery.

We realised that when Paul had written to the church in Corinth, he was thinking of a loftier connection[1], but for us community life was at times very physical. This became more so when Aelred was the first of our number to become incontinent. You could smell him coming in the corridor. What to do? Brother Anthony, who was then Infirmarian, told Chapter he considered this to be part of his duties.

'To a certain point,' said Father Abbot. 'But you cannot be expected to bear this burden alone. It is a new development—indeed, an insight perhaps to our future—in the life of the order. We need to learn what to do to help you and', only just realising Aelred was among us, 'and Brother Aelred, of course.' It was perhaps the only time Aelred could have been considered a pacesetter.

1. 1 Corinthians 12:12-26

Overheard from one guest to another as they left chapel: 'If they spend so much time in silence, why do so many of them need to wear hearing aids?'

Though We Are Many

Father Martin's crack came at the Offertory during the community Eucharist. He had had his senior moments—we all had—such as when at the ablutions he filled the chalice with wine rather than using a little water. He felt compelled to drink it, believing it to have had contact with the blood of Christ. Having a drunk monk who was supposed to be cooking lunch was a gift the community could have done without that day.

The Visitor was traditionally the local diocesan bishop. That was until we found ourselves in the pastoral care of a pompous prelate in purple, who loved to hold aloft his episcopal ring as he approached you. Some of our number would go down on one knee and kiss the badge of office on the proffered hand. The bishop clearly got more out of the encounter than we did. After his first visit Father Abbot sought Chapter's agreement to amend the Rule, as he told us had been done by some radical nuns in Haggerston in East London, to allow us to select our own Visitor.

Before adopting this variation, the Visitor came into the Refectory and Fr Martin stood by the door, part of the discipline involved in being Brother Kitchen. The bishop stopped, elevated his hand to Martin, who sank to one knee, which gave way and he kept going, collapsing on the floor, taking with him the Visitor, whose face was now the colour of his cassock. The meal was strained after that, especially as Father Abbot had lifted the traditional silence in honour of our guest. Never was Grace after a meal so heartily offered.

The day of enlightenment as to Martin's state of mind followed our sharing of the Peace. The brother came forward with the bread and the wine for the mass. Martin looked at him enquiringly. Michael held the gifts slightly higher. Martin nodded. Father Abbot came forward, took the first of the elements contained in the ciborium, placed it on the altar and proceeded to fill the chalice. That too he placed on the corporal. Martin stood immobile. The abbot whispered in Martin's ear. Another blank look, then a dawning of awareness. He lifted the elements and recited the Offertory prayers, and the mass proceeded without incident until the ablutions. It was a foretaste of the broken love that community living entails.

Found myself laughing during a hymn at St Matthew's Sunday service. It was 'Let All Mortal Flesh Keep Silence'. It is really a beautiful hymn, but I can never erase the memory of three monks, after a bean supper, all farting loudly at the same time as they as they bowed to the Blessed Sacrament in chapel during Exposition. It has that effect—laughter—every time I hear it.

Packing Up

'Just take what you need,' he said.

I nodded.

'The bare necessities.' This time he barked.

No doubt it was to shake me out of the overwhelming confusion that must have appeared on my face when the Chair of Trustees had asked, 'What would you like to take with you?'

It was this question that sparked the frozen panic. Was I, a lay brother, being asked what were the treasures of St Candida's? Was I the custodian of goods as well as tradition?

I thought of all the beautiful furniture, especially those crafted by Father Augustine, the cabinet maker who had a vision, as Joseph and Jesus before him, that timber could be turned into beauty for the use of the devout. His talents complemented those of Brother Kentigern, whose delicate carvings could be found dotted around the House—small Calvaries, angels and the Blessed Mother, surprising little animals under the misericords in the chapel, and his masterpiece, the Stations of the Cross—tiny reminders to the brethren and visitors that while we live in this place, our homeland is in heaven.

The letter to the Philippians tells us that in word, but two members of our community did so in wood.

The Chair was in business, well regarded, a member of the House of Lords no less, who had somehow combined commercial ruthlessness with religious compassion. No doubt the latter was being brought to bear as I looked at him, unable to respond to his enquiry.

The monastery was greatly blessed with religious artefacts, objects of devotion, gorgeously rendered items made by members of the community or donated to it. They were in a way, like the BCP definition of a sacrament, outward and visible signs of inward and spiritual grace. Was it now up to me to decide what was to survive?

'Just take what you need: habits, summer and winter. Clothing, shoes, et cetera. That goes without saying. But what else do you need?'

'An Office book each. A Bible.'

'Good. That's the spirit. Travel light.' I realised the Chair's questions were more immediate than pastoral. Of course, the Trustees had overseen the compilation of a detailed inventory, from which sales, donations and collections would ensue to support the life of what would replace St Candida's.

I was reminded that the community, through the agency of Father Abbot, had placed all authority for the disposal of the estate to the care of the Trustees. My first business encounter with the Chair—as distinct from the times he had been a guest on retreat—was when I was summoned to a meeting of the Trustees in Father Abbot's parlour. Fr Aidan was not present.

'Look, Columba, let's not beat about the bush. You know we are proceeding in accordance with Chapter's decision made when you were a little farther back in the unfolding plot of Agatha Christie...'

I looked blank. I often do with people who speak around the topic.

'*And Then There Were None*,' chipped in a smart-suited woman. 'At least, I think that is still the accepted, if not acceptable, title.'

A titter went round the room.

'So the Trustees are of a mind to ensure that this community is represented in its decisions…look, I know the Abbot is an ex-officio member of the Board, but we all know that his…', the Chair paused delicately, '…his mental faculties are no longer quite what they were. The foundation documents state that the Abbot must be in priest's orders and that he is ex-officio a Trustee. But the time has come for pragmatism.'

It was at this point that I thanked the Board, pleading that my experience in the garden, kitchen, laundry, culminating in the dizzy heights of being Guestmaster, did not really fit me for such important decisions. I told them I trusted them to ensure that whatever decisions they made on the future of the Community of Saint Candida's treasures—I could not bring myself to replicate the Board's use of the word 'assets'—they would be the best equipped for the task.

I was interrupted by the Chair. He assured me that both Father Aidan and I would be appropriately cared for—finances were sufficiently good for that—and that the accrued benefits of the sale of the monastery, its goods and the like, would be used strictly in accordance with the vision of The Founder.

I chose two Calvaries, in different woods and from different periods of Brother Kentigern's work, a small icon of Our Lady written by an Oblate and given to the House, and a prie-dieu each for Aidan and me, the handiwork of Father Augustine. (The second prie-dieu turned out to be a mistake.

The Abbot, whose physical powers were beginning to come into alignment with his mental ones, could not make the journey to his knees, even if he had thought to do so.[1])

So it was with our clothing. Sorry, Lord, we did take a cloak and a change of shoes but, by Imelda Marcos standards, it was nothing. I added *The Cloud of Unknowing*, ensuring it was a version that included *The Book of Privy Counsel*, Julian of Norwich and Teresa of Avila's *The Interior Castle* to the pile of books. As for the rest of the library, which I knew included several valuable and collectible items, I have no idea what happened to them. The Chair assured me that those which could find appropriate homes would, but reasserted that it was the duty of the Trustees to ensure a good return on the assets of the monastery to ensure all costs pertaining to the care of the Abbot and myself could be met, as well as whatever was established in the spirit of The Founder's vision.

It seems ironic that what was a vision of flowering growth—and the Community of Saint Candida did flourish—is now on the wane. I bristle at times that the responsibility for overseeing the extinction—supervised, of course, by the able and gifted Trustees—had come down to me.

Yet Qoheleth gives counsel: 'In the morning sow your seed, and at evening withhold not your hand; for you do not know which will prosper, this or that, or whether both alike will be good.'[2]

1. The redundant prie-dieu now sits in my study in the Rectory. It gets about as much use, shamefully on my part, as it would have if it had stayed in Father Aidan's room. Though it does come in handy for the use by a penitent now and then.

2. Ecclesiastes 11:6. Columba has unusually drawn on the Revised Standard Version.

Papering Over The Past

The Trustees, I learned, were equally as focussed when it came to archiving paper as they were to the rest of the House's contents. The books of the library were sent out to interested parties—though the would-be recipients of the benefaction proved to be selective. Monks wrote a lot of books. I suppose they had the time to do so. When the books were printed they made their way to shelves of communities like St Candida's. While our collection was unusual to the wider world, it was not to those who store or sell such material. Not all literature stands the test of time, and so it was with our holy musings.

Fr Aidan's papers were different. They were eagerly taken up by his old college. His personal storehouse, despite the monastic ideal to sit light to belongings and the passing fancies of the world, was extensive. He had been given a storeroom by the Abbot who recognised the young monk's gifts. This treasure trove had in earlier days been kept in obsessively chronicled detail. This oversight had slipped somewhat over the years as Fr Aidan's health and mind declined.

The face of the archivist from his *alma mater* broke into joy when she saw how much original material lay in Fr Abbot's store. She also noted that despite the slapdash nature of latter storage, that from earlier times was a pointer not only to Aidan's thoughts, but his methods. I expect some doctoral student will be crawling over them to pay homage to the many faceted life of Fr Aidan: priest, academic, monk, abbot. Before the catholic movement tottered towards minusculinity such a book would have been a highlight in the publishing world. Reviews would have featured in the secular press, but now would be lucky to get a mention in the Church Times. But with the seemingly relentless rise of shiny new church, and the marginality that religious publishing seems to inhabit, any work on Father Abbot will at best probably find a home in a small academic publisher's list.

'It's good to know Fr Aidan's intellectual contributions are going to be returning to their place of germination,' the Chair said.

'Father Abbot's home was here. He came here as a young man to pray and focus his life, and others', on God,' I said.

'Yes, yes.'

And in the same way the disposal of the monastery furniture was settled, a team of packers arrived to take the contents of Aidan's room to be sifted, catalogued and kept.

'We can provide you with a copy,' the archivist, a bright eyed woman in her thirties, said.

'He won't have room for that.' It was the Chair. 'He is going to a single room in a care home.'

She looked at me with concern.

'No. Father Abbot and I are going together. It's a way of keeping the Order intact.'

'It could be digital. It would fit on a small stick. Eventually, I hope, it will be online anyway. So all you would need is a computer.'

'No need for that,' said the Chair. 'Columba is not an academic. The garden, the kitchen, the guest wing, that was more your thing, wasn't it, Brother?' He smiled.

'And the chapel,' I said. I could feel the blush on my cheeks as soon as I spoke. An uncomfortable silence followed. 'He was a great thinker. An inspiration,' I said.

'Yes. A terrible shame,' said the Chair. 'Still, I suppose it comes to us all.'

The archivist looked at me in sympathy.

'Please look after it well,' I said.

She nodded. 'We will.'

And I walked away.

Whither The
Still Small Voice?

My mind is aclatter. So much of what I took for routine has been reconfigured that I struggle to find a rhythm. Meal times in Care Home are aspirational. And yet they are when we seek to find community but, because of the varying physical and mental powers of the residents, is more a procession of competing attentions—sought, accommodated or denied—as the carers (though some of them at times seem to struggle to grasp the concept in their job title), family members and, in Fr Aidan's case, me, seek to cajole, assist or almost resort to compulsion to get the residents to eat.

The quest for a rhythm to the day is likewise an objective: get up, change clothes, get others up, change them into what accords with their various bodily capacities—there is a lot of nappy wearing in a care home—feed them, get some activity going for those who will accept it, feed them, change clothes, engage in another activity, feed them, change them, put them to bed.

In many ways the monastic routine was similar, though the monks, by and large, were able to do much of it for themselves. (I had never served as Infirmarian. Those who did tended not to gossip about what the post entailed.) What transformed the potential deadness of monotony in the monastery was the added extra—no, the core of our life together—of prayer and worship. Much of that is impossible here.

Not that outside the home affords a clearer prospect. The haphazard, random, joyful and occasionally desperate seem to jockey for position in which no order or hierarchy can be discerned. It is hard to accept, but I have come to realise that so much of my life has been contained and controlled by discipline. I was going to say that this was in the best possible way. How could I know or be the judge of that? Such judgment, in the absence of a functional superior, is for God.

A great part of my life is the result of a chance gift. Or, more accurately, grace. Abandoned (rescued?) and recovered (or am I still recovering?) from excess of disorder led me to perhaps an excess of regularity. Now here in the home and less so on the streets of this community—how odd it feels to use that word about anything other than the company of men with whom I have shared so much of life, still do in a fresh expression, with Father Aidan here—I seek to find the pattern that holds a common life together.

The distillation of this task is its united efforts. The centrifugal power of decay—people, places, and now even memory—makes for solitariness. The monk on his own, like Anthony in the desert, is not what I had imagined for myself. I had found life with brethren.

So I struggled to maintain the routine of the cloister, as I read the offices with, or more accurately to, Fr Aidan. Now and then he sparks: the Benedictus, the Magnificat, the Nunc Dimmitis, the Lord's Prayer, sometimes even the odd psalm in its entirety, albeit from Coverdale in the 1662 Book of Common

Prayer instead of the text of *Common Worship* being held in my hands—a change he oversaw as Abbot—will cascade from mind to tongue. But most days the round of prayer seems like a cry in the desert, a potsherd, as a man chants to his brother in the hope that the other will join him in praise of his Father.

The jangle of television sounds from competing stations, incessant assistance alarm calls that could suggest residents are being ignored (they are not; some residents have something of a propensity for hitting the button for any reason or, sometimes out of a desire for some human contact—I have heard carers calling this behaviour as 'bell happy'), the buzz of the front doorbell, radios, music in common areas gives a bedrock of cacophony. Aidan seems to have found an ability to ignore it all. Not surprising, I suppose, as some would think he ignores me, but then they have never witnessed the fretting that quickly escalates to agitation if I seek solace outside the confines of the home, or even his room—not that there is much silent solace to be found there.

I am considering asking the manager for a small plot of ground. But conversations with some of the staff have not proved promising. Yes, I could probably be allowed to do some digging, but flowers are discouraged. They remind residents of death—dare I say that I would have thought just looking at each other was reminder enough? The argument given me was that the only blooms that make their way here are usually leftovers from a funeral. What about birthdays, Mothering Sunday, other events? (I have a sneaking suspicion it may be the extra work and oversight, beyond many of the residents, that would fall to the carers that is the driving force behind the discouragement.)

I countered this by expressing a preference for vegetables.

After all, as Brother Gardener I was for a while the main producer of the monastery's non-meat provender. That would not work either, says one of them, there being strict regulations about what food can be prepared on site. Surely, then, an exception could be made? A condescendingly pitiful shake of the head greets this. Couldn't I give just give it to the staff and visitors? A consultation between some of them follows. This throws them: something they can use, and free. It might be possible but permission would have to be sought from higher up the management life-chain.

So much of my time for prayer and reflection, I realise, has come through work—in the garden, in the kitchen, in running the Guest Wing. St Benedict said to work is to pray. No work risks no prayer. What life is there for me now? Of course, accompanying Father Aidan *is* my work. But what happens when he is no longer? Which, in a way, he already is.

In Thought, Word and Deed[1] Wash Me Throughly—3

Every day I say I am sorry. To God. To others: the fellow residents and workers here in Care Home; and my brothers— Fr Abbot, but also those who are no longer with us. Sometimes I even say sorry to myself. This repeated three-way practice is so ingrained that, by virtue of our move to Bethnal Green, I sometimes worry that I am spiritually beyond the pale.

That may sound extreme. But the repeated acknowledgement of one's shortcomings and failings is liberating. Though I have had to learn that such an experience is far from universal.

At CSC there were two collective points where members of the community would resort to confession—at the beginning of the Eucharist and at the start of Compline. That these came at either end of the day gave a certain symmetry to our gatherings. To undergird the reflective importance of this discipline a period of silence would be kept.

A guest once asked me, with a seeming sense of puzzlement, about these pauses.

'You spend most of the day in silence. Why on earth, in some of the few times you come together to speak...'

'To pray.'

'Okay, to pray. But you do it in words, though. Spoken words. Why on earth do you stop for another silence?'

This had never before seemed strange to me. That we should pause to consider how we might have offended God or brethren was, to me, only sensible. I have been to many churches—fortunately, the local one is not among these—where the priest says something like, 'Let us call to mind our sins,' only to launch straight into 'Almighty God' or whatever form of confession they use with hardly a pause for intake of breath, let alone calling to mind.

I responded to the guest, 'But that is personal silence. A corporate silence...' He looked puzzled. '...by that I mean one we come together to share, is different. And it has a specific purpose. Confession is at the heart of our faith. And forgiveness.'

Others, I know, worry that this practice is simply a meaningless repetitive routine by rote. Or worse, an institutional abuse, a system by which appropriate self-esteem is repeatedly undercut: each time one of us starts to enjoy the air of freedom, one's head is plunged beneath the water of self-contempt.

It is undeniably true that some people have suffered, and probably still do, under the tyranny of the sacrament of reconciliation from put-downs that may have been too harshly interpreted. At times I fear I myself have not heard the forgiveness extended by a priest. Or maybe I hold on to some of my failings because of their badness? That part of my past is ultimately beyond the pale. Is there a healthy attitude to this admission of our shortcomings and failures? The Novice Master was adamant in this.

'Don't think this is just about you. When we pause to check the state of lives, we do so collectively. Our brotherhood is then coming together—yes, and there will be things on your conscience alone—to confess those sins in thought, word and deed. But never consider yourself the speck of dirt in the middle of the universe that cannot be cleaned. That is why it is a community event, confession. In a way we acknowledge we are part of the universal. Sin is personal, collective, societal, communal, corporate, national and global. Arguably universal. "If we say we have no sin we deceive ourselves and the truth is not in us."[2] So this practice is one of acknowledgment of what it is like to be human. "To err is human. To forgive is Godly."[3]'

I can't remember the precise time I discerned a shift in my consciousness of moving from the concept of myself as a doer of sins to *being* a sinner. It is not that I am worthless— far from it, I am not evil; indeed, I am a loved child of God. In my experience only a tiny number of people could ever be considered evil. And then, as Fr Abbot would say, who are we to judge?

In some ways—and how perverse it seems to write this—an awareness of sin is a state of grace. Knowing we are not perfect, and never can be, frees us to give praise to that unstoppable outpouring of love we call God.

In the confession we used at the conventual mass—and I was glad to see that it forms part of the liturgy, at least for festivals and ordinary time, at St Matthew's—there are two threefold aspects. The first is the sin itself. Or, arguably, what causes sin—negligence, weakness and our own deliberate fault.[4] The first and third of these seem blameworthy. But weakness? I remember a saying—was it from the 1970s? — 'the devil made me do that.'[5] It seems a little too convenient. But weakness is hardly devilment.

The Novice Master gave an extended lesson in discerning sin once. He was at pains to get his charges to understand that temptation, while not healthy, is not necessarily sinful. It is what flows from it. 'Temptation is an indicator of the leaning of the heart. Jesus repeatedly tells us that it is what flows from the heart, not from keeping a set of rules, that is paramount. Temptation can lead to sin, yes. So we must be on our guard. But it may not constitute the sin itself.' Which, strangely, left us a little bewildered in trying to tell the difference.

And there is the other three: thought, word and deed. Simple enough, you might think. But—and, as they say, there is always a but—how do we count our sins of thought? Word— saying intentionally, even accidentally, hurtful things—needs to be admitted. It is best, of course, done face to face. But that is not always possible. The person you offended may have moved on, been encountered randomly, or even have died. Word I understand. And deed.

But thought? What constitutes sinful thinking? One novice was clear: it was about lust. That seemed too specific and unfair. And, I suppose, ultimately crippling. Lustful thoughts, though regrettable, are surely only sinful when a deed follows. This is about understanding the difference between temptation and transgression. Or am I being naïve?

Perhaps so. Because if I am honest, I am sometimes crippled by thoughts of sin. Or the sins that have been, or may have been, committed because of my sinful thoughts. As a human, surely no action or utterance is possible without thought? It may be unconscious. It may come from a deep well of repression, but there must be thought there somewhere.

As so much sin, so much of my sin, is thoughtful. I recall—sometimes I almost experience a physical twinge—the thoughtless (do I mean that? Haven't I just written that no sin can be without thought?) actions I have done. At the time with Marian it did not seem that our actions were bad. It just seemed natural. But, as my father said, we had ventured into dangerous waters. And so we were expelled from our fools' paradise. And Donna, fearful of each physical approach, the last tantamount to assault. How will they ever know the remorse, the regret, the repeated times I have tried to repent of those events?

Once, during confession, the monk said to me, 'Brother, how often do you think you need to confess a sin?' He had obviously heard me speak of the matter before.

'I don't know, Father. Isn't it seventy-seven times? Or seventy times seven?'[6]

'That is about others, as I am sure you know. I want you to go away and read John's account of the raising of Lazarus. "Unbind him and let him go."[7] That is what Jesus says. And, if you want to walk in the loving grace that God gives to us, you must accept, you must take hold of, the loving release in this sacrament. After absolution I say, "Rejoice and be glad. The Lord has put away your sin. Go in peace." You are unbound, Brother. But you must also let go.'

I have thought about that a lot.

---

1. I have taken the liberty here of linking this section to the other ones by the Coverdale Psalm reference in the subtitle. Columba's title is simply *In Thought, Word and Deed*.

2. 1 John 1:8

3. This a variant of 'To err is humane; to forgive is divine', attributed to Alexander Pope in his *An Essay on Criticism*.

4. This comes from one of the confessions in Order One of the Eucharist in *Common Worship*, the authorised services used in the Church of England.

5. A common enough phrase, but I wonder—I have no proof for this—if he is drawing on the American comedian Flip Wilson, who used to get a laugh by using just that catchphrase. It seems unlikely that it never it made it to the United Kingdom.

6. Columba's self-quoted response draws on Jesus's question to Peter in Matthew 18:22.

7. The extensive account of the raising of Lazarus appears in John's gospel, Chapter 11. The quote, 'Unbind him and let him go' is John 11:44.

The Narrow Door

The cord has snapped.

As I sit in Fr Aidan's room, I realise now that my anxieties about the end of community life are groundless. In one way our common life died the day we left the enclosure. It had also, does also, cease to be when Fr Aidan, God love him, fails to recognise the rhythm of prayer he has given his life to. Or me.

Our residence here is no more than it should be—two ageing men, one of whom requires care somewhat beyond the capacities of the other—are easing in the process of leaving the earth.

The monastery, beautiful as it was, was the mere shell that held the daily round of prayer and work. The fellowship of the brothers, the routine of praise and contemplation, the repetitive and creative tasks the monks gave their time and talents to, are all held in the confines of adopted seclusion.

Having left those confines, the task for me—in the company, rather than under the guidance, of Fr Aidan, even though he remains my superior—is to seek a way of faithful service. I pray God will assist me in that task, and give me grace to discern what form my life will take in the future, as I expect I shall survive Fr Abbot's death as I have his mental decline.

> I thought 'I shall die in my own house,
> my days as numerous as the grains of sand.'[1]

This was not to be. But, like Job, I need to press on, as he does in his discourse:

> 'My roots spread out to the waters,
> with the dew all night on my branches;
> my glory was fresh with me,
> and my bow ever new in my hand.'[2]

1. Job 2:18. This translation is from the New International Version, at variance to much of the quotations from Columba who uses, as many 'modern' catholics do, the New Revised Standard Version. After some discussion with the staff at Care Home, I learned that the Gideons had placed Bibles in the home. It may be assumed, then, that Columba was using one of them when he penned this piece.
2. Job 29:19-20. For some reason Brother Columba reverts to his usual custom of using the NRSV.

Not With A Bang

Much of my early life with CSC was spent in discernment. For my brothers, this seemed often an urgent and energy-consuming task. I tended to drift, not through laziness, but, after the shock of arrival, I realised there was much to unravel—and, no doubt, to dry out from some intense experiences of drink and dope. (Even dissolution seemed more innocent then.)

The recipe was simple. Lots of time in quiet. This could be used in many ways—in the daily tasks the Novice Master gave us (though in the days after my arrival I was master of my own time; I was far from being considered a potential recruit.)

It was some weeks before I drifted into chapel. What I encountered there evoked a mixture of intrigue and revulsion. A waft of incense, an infectious calm, a kind of comforting danger lurking in the darkness, a couple of silent forms in stalls and one of the floor. It was the beginning of a beckoning, a connecting, a reconnecting with a hidden or, so I had thought, forgotten heritage; or perhaps the beginning of an uncoupling from the false exterior I had come to know as me.

As I eased into a new calm, digging in the garden, collecting fruit from the orchard, weeding, collecting and arranging flowers—much of my initiation was in the open air—I found myself asking myself the question, 'What are you going to do with your life?'

The focus of concentration at some stage moved inside, both of buildings and myself. The still of the chapel had a seductive quality; it seemed a place that had a siren voice. The monks there in prayer/contemplation/meditation moved from threat to invitation to do no more than join them in silence. The calm was tinged with contagion. Yet the calm that beckoned me seemed to increase even when there was no-one in the chapel. Stillness began to call me and, in time, become part of me.

My vocation has been a quiet one. After the frenetic enjoyment—did I really enjoy it? or was I simply seeking to join in some generational mummery?—of Kombi life, driving through Europe, enjoying the sights, sounds, tastes, smells and feel of places and people (generally and intimately), I found myself, like Jonah vomited on a beach by the big fish, in a new land. St Candida's seemed to be my Nineveh.

I realise I have shifted the perspective of the prophet from subject to object. In all this I sensed a call to repentance. As in much of God's work, this was not sudden—I have never been a great lover of road to Damascus conversion stories—but a slow, yet hardly smooth, yet still remarkably quiet journey.

Each generation is accused of claiming the discovery of sex, and mine was no exception, apart from the noise we seemed to generate about it. And the recently won freedom to indulge in what some commentators mistakenly thought as condemnatory, as copulation without complications—clearly meant only in the physical sense of moving to conception. Emotions seemed just as complex, whatever we claimed. We also seemed to have made much about social confrontations— politics and values that allowed more 'freedom', justice (while, at the same time, fostering the rise of the mega-corporation) and meditation. It was a heady or even possibly toxic mix.

Of course, any such discovery or invention is illusory: we are, as the hymn goes, pilgrims on a journey.[1] How we take our steps is a dialogue in movement, of our own and God's. My feet found security in a path that, in some ways, was a well worn one. It was, however, one that was fairly new to the Church of England, and had been part of the vision of The Founder, along with the proliferation of religious orders throughout the country that attended the Oxford Movement, one that had a life cycle. (As all things do.)

The quiet of Saint Candida's allowed me to grow and, in doing so with many priests, brothers and visitors, it opened up a vista of contemplation. I was never gifted with great insights. I could not teach like Fr Aidan; I did not have the handiwork skills of Fr Augustine; I lacked the musical prowess of successive Brothers Music; no healing touch essential to the Infirmarian had been laid on me.

What I had was a chance to turn. There was a dawn of something beyond myself and my desires. I had been dumped after overindulging myself in ephemeral pastimes that had inflicted terrible damage on others. So many people were due—and are still, to my mind—repeated apologies because of my selfishness. Have I deluded myself in thinking confession to God would absolve me from any personal damage I inflicted on other people? I have quietly sought to fulfil my vocation: a quiet thank you to God in harmony with the quiet choirs in eternity.

1. Columba is referring to Richard A. M. Gillard's *The Servant Song.*

Ringing The Changes

Bells. At first they were an exotic irritant, calling me from slumber and an unrecognised withdrawal from alcohol and dope. They punctuated the day with meaning for the monks; with bewilderment for me.

In time I came to discern them: the initial brisk alarum that rang out at five in the morning, rousing those who were not up already (to my astonishment, once I too could manage being upright at that hour, the number was small—many were already at their private devotions in the chapel, to which the remnant made their way); the prolonged peal calling the brothers to mass; the curt summons to meals; and, mother of all them, the Angelus.

The day was spun on a web around the Angelus. At six in the morning, at noon and again six hours later, we stopped what we were doing when we heard the chimed pattern of three bells three times, followed by a conjoined nine—recalling in ring God's plan to draw the Blessed Virgin Mary out of ordinariness to be the mother of Himself in Jesus.

The pattern had a seasonal variation. From Easter to Ascension the bells rang out in a different pattern—the separated three sets of three becoming a single nine—at the same times to invoke a different observance, the Regina Coeli, joining in Mary's joy at the fulfilment of her Son's redemption of the world.

As my understanding grew of what the various bells meant, so did a realisation that I was somehow becoming part of the common life at St Candida's. I found myself drawn into the web of devotion that kept these men going in their dignified routine.

Some time into my residence, after I had put myself forward as a possible recruit to their ranks, I was inducted into the code of sounds. When I moved from postulant to novice I was given the responsibility for ringing the Angelus. Such a simple task at first had a jangling effect on my nerves. You had to be in church, at the end of the rope before the chapel clock ticked to its chime of the hour. As soon as it started to ring, you pulled the rope. Missing this duty was unthinkable.

When duties were reallocated by the abbot, the bell ringer is was always pivotal post. As we started to crumble in numbers, memory and vitality, I found myself again given the duty of alerting the diminishing number of brothers to the wonder of Christ's salvation, and its honouring of His mother. It hurts to think that bell no longer rings, let alone echoes itself in prayer.

The Rhythm Method

So much of monastic life takes its power from the pattern of the day. For some people—at least, from what I have learned from conversations with some first-time retreatants in my role as Guestmaster—there is both allure and aversion in the monastery timetable.

Visitors would sometimes tell me, with an urgency bordering on desperation, how they could never live to such a rule. They see a kind of tyranny in what appears to them as so much repetition.

Each day, each office, each moment has something different to offer. Spiritual direction is not—never has been—one of my gifts, so I would arrange for guests to see other members of the order who had what I lacked.

All I can point to, from my own experience, is the wonder that can be found in limiting oneself to a reduced range of experiences. This could, I suppose, reflect a lack of adventurousness.

Visitors were the stuff of life for a Guestmaster. It was a quaintly formal job, receiving requests from Vicarages, Rectories and Parsonages on headed notepaper, the writer asking if space and time could be afforded them for a prayerful break. Securing a date at certain times of year was risky. Many clergymen—and it was only clergymen then—favoured early spring, as the countryside began to awaken. The exigencies of Easter expended, before the arrival of curates, seeking space to consider the future, they headed to St Candida's to recuperate, reactivate and relax.

Nearly all, in the early days, arrived by public transport and wearing cassocks. Over the years we had to extend our minimal car parking facilities, and the clergy daywear evaporated. I would enquire if they had been with us before. Sometimes I could recall or tell without asking, as many were repeat offenders. We could almost calculate to the day the dates for the following year's stay as they left. For newcomers, and some who had not been for some time, I would give an orientation: Chapel here, quiet in the cloister, silence over meals, hours of the offices and the mass, Greater Silence, and my maps of walks.

Regulars needed little reminding of the routine. New or old, we usually lost them for the first day or so. After the (re-) acquaintance tour, they would retire to their cell and sleep. The gentle, or far from it, snoring would ring out along the halls. A few—not many—would head out for a bracing first day yomp.

After the initial activity—or lack of it—a new pattern would emerge. A few would spend their days scouring the shelves of the library taking notes, writing books, rejuvenating their intellects ignored or put aside because of the pressures of priestly duties. A couple would sit in the guests' parlour reading what looked like trashy novels. Some would spend all day in the Chapel in prayer and meditation. Others would strap on their boots and go out for walks. They would not be seen except for meals. My predecessor said a retreat was a time when we could allow these men to be the kind of priest they really wanted to be.

Whatever they did, these priests, for the most part, looked refreshed at the end of their stay. Eyes brightened, muscles strained or relaxed, and they returned to the parish or chaplaincy with a renewed vigour and, occasionally, a reluctance to face the round of petty squabbles they had temporarily fled. In some was a discernible reluctance to immerse themselves back into that which had delivered them here in exhaustion. Some expressed the desire to stay. But they knew, as we did, that this was illusory. Being a monk was a burden in a different way.

A guest to the Guestmaster (not me): 'On the first day I am exhausted. On the second I am recovering. On the third day, I can enter into the swing of things. I always want to join you on the third day. I mean, permanently. As a monk. By the end I realise I would drive you—or you would drive me—crazy.'

Guestmaster to guest: 'Ah, yes. Discernment.'

Ruins and Boundaries

On that final journey with Donna, as I had in other parts of Britain and Ireland, we seemed to specialise in ruins: abbeys, priories, monasteries, convents. The more managed and promoted—Fountains, Riveaulx, Tintern, Whitby, Glastonbury—always got a steady stream of visitors. Some, particularly in Ireland, were off the usual tourist track. A hand painted sign would direct you to a house where you could get a key to the gate to allow admission.

These places were ideal to pull up the Kombi. Quiet, relatively remote, a watchful though respectful neighbour, meant we could count on a good night's sleep, or a secluded trysting spot. As a monk I sometimes wonder if what we enjoyed in those places was tantamount to blasphemy. I put it to Fr Aidan once.

'Sadly, Brother, I don't think so. I think blasphemy only counts in the heart and mind of a believer. For someone outside the community of faith the Lord's name, for instance, is not being taken in vain. It is though our boundaries don't exist.'

Yet boundaries form so much of the cloistered life. Silences, rooms and wings of restricted access—none more than an individual's cell—were various forms of delineation. Some were obvious—what else could the sign Community Only mean? So much of our routine, presaged by bells—prayer, meditation, work, recreation—was an embodiment of restriction, but with a higher purpose.

These very definitions were captured in our titles: Brother, Father. CSC would have to have been the last community insisting on titles that differentiated between lay and ordained members.

Fences. Around the boundary of the monastery's property. And demarcation within. The gardens had fences. They were either open, or restricted to the community—though many a guest stumbled into both. There were barriers around the workshops, walls around the drying area.

As the community's numbers thinned I began to see my crumbling brothers as a kind of ruins. Those for whom forgetfulness was the only reminder of life; the abandonment of a lifetime's profession.

Fr Abbot once decided to introduce an aperitif before our Thursday supper. Lunch was the main meal which, in honour of the Last Supper, was already enhanced by a glass of wine. The idea was to exchange the feastly quality of the day by replacing the wine at lunch with a small drink in the evening.

The festive element was not as celebratory as you might think. Poor Br Cecil particularly struggled with this. In a seeming gesture of largesse, he would give his lunchtime glass (or distribute its contents in parts) to other brothers at the Refectory table. This was not strictly within the spirit of the celebration: to each a joy, shared by commonality. But by doing this he managed to avoid putting alcohol to his lips.

Fr Abbot, not long after his election, noticed this. He called

Br Cecil in for a long chat. At the next meeting of Chapter I noticed the absence of Br Cecil. When the abbot called us to order, he explained that Cecil was a reformed alcoholic. The Thursday festal enhancement was an ongoing torture for him. He did not want to draw attention to himself in this, yet he felt he could not, indeed must not, partake of the wine. He suffered the discomfort, as we all must, for the sake of the community.

Fr Abbot also explained that Br Cecil had taken to subterfuge at mass: while he appeared to drink our Lord's blood from the chalice he was, in fact, doing his level best to avoid wine coming into contact with his lips, let alone take some into his mouth.

Here, Fr Abbot, said, was a case of the ear and the toe.[1] First, the community's priests were reminded that reception of holy communion was sufficient in one kind, solid or liquid. Was it not the blessing of the cup a sharing in Christ's blood?[2] No-one, he said, should be forced to take both. (As Guestmaster I was later to advise Coeliacs that the Precious Blood alone was indeed a full partaking of Holy Communion. We had never heard of gluten-free wafers.)

So, for an experimental period, wine would be served as an optional aperitif at supper. We would take our places in the Refectory and the lector would be replaced by a monk who delivered a short talk. The abbot reasoned that a concentrated bit of intellectual input should accompany the wine. Delivery of the talk would be done by rotation. Some members of the community seemed unnerved that this may fall to them. At the end we would proceed with the meal.

The experiment was not a success. The easy taking of wine during a meal was superseded by a self-conscious slurping, some brothers gulping, others slowly savouring each sip. After about a month the project was abandoned. All meals, until the sudden death of Cecil a couple of years later—a heart attack while digging up potatoes in the garden—were dry. A cruel irony, perhaps, was that wine with meals was reintroduced on the day of his funeral.

One aspect of the accompaniment of aperitif—the short talk—remains with me. Fr Aidan was speaking. Like his sermons, much learning seemed to be concentrated into a short space. In the allotted fifteen minutes Fr Aidan spoke of the movement from the eremitic life to the coenobitic. It was, he said, tantamount to a removal of a singular temptation. Pachomius had effectively overseen the bringing together of solitaries into a community. As communities emerged there came the need for regulation: what has come to be known as a Rule.

Men and women had long been on a solo journey—a life of denial in which they sought to deepen their awareness of their need of God. Some, such as the stylites, went to extremes. The most famous of these was, of course, Simon. His journey was both spiritually and physically stretching. The platform he began on was a mere four feet above the ground. In time it grew—Lord knows how, nor did Fr Aidan enlighten us—to sixty.

St Basil thought the solitary life was fraught with temptations. Initially seeking salvation by prayer and repentance in isolation, without the distraction of human company, these hermits single-handedly sought to earn God's loving forgiveness.

But, as Fr Aidan pointed out, Basil saw the pitfalls. The idiorhythmic life could easily become one of self-obsession. The path to God was replaced by absorption with one's own body, mind or spirit. So Basil prescribed communities. They grew to huge numbers, walled cities of men and women, seeking a common life. Not all were successful. Nor were all that holy.

So the Rule came to provide a framework for behaviour. By the time it got to Benedict, perhaps the guiding light of monastic regulation, nearly all aspects of life inside and beyond the chapel came to have guidelines and instructions. And the Abbot is the guardian of the Rule.

What happens when Fr Aidan dies? I will be alone. Does that invalidate my membership of the brotherhood of CSC? Who will oversee me? Are the boundaries of my life destined to be replaced by ruins, if not of the monastery buildings, but the ghosts of my associates? I am sure the Robed Buddhists will care for the monastery, whatever adaptations they consider necessary, but what is a monk's life without fellowship? I must ensure some new kind of community replaces the one crumbling here in Care Home.

At times I imagine myself a living ruin—the only remaining moving habit of CSC in the world. (That is not fair, of course. Most days we do get Fr Abbot into his for at least part of the day.) I am like an animated robot, the kind favoured by museums and country houses in the 1980s—of limited movement, but with a short introductory commentary which sought to bring the artifice 'alive'.

I recall an early philosophical conundrum that the Novice Master once used to whet our intellectual appetites for Thomas Aquinas. I know now that even then it was well-worn. If a tree falls over in a forest and nobody witnesses it, would the event be real if it were unknown? I think we were supposed to explore the limits or otherwise of objectivity.

Certainly, if things continue as they are, I will see the fall of the oak that is Fr Abbot, and along with him, the forest that was the Community of Saint Candida. But what about me?

1. A reference in a somewhat distorted rendering to the body metaphor used in 1 Corinthians 12.

2. 1 Corinthians 10:16

Tick-Tock

It is the ticking of the clock I miss. Or clocks. One in the chapel, in the entrance lobby, the Chapter House and one in the Refectory. They must have come as a job lot, each unique but of similar age and construction.

The clock had a gentle click that reminded us that, whatever our own desires, time was passing. Some guests found it oppressive, a needless disturbance of otherwise peaceful surroundings. But for me it had a cadence of wisdom, not so much Marvell's 'time's wingèd chariot' as Qoheleth's:

I have seen the business that God has given to everyone to be busy with. He has made everything suitable for its time; moreover, he has put a sense of past and future into their minds, yet they cannot find out what God has done from the beginning to the end. I know that there is nothing better for them than to be happy and enjoy themselves as long as they live; moreover, it is God's gift that all should eat and drink and take pleasure in all their toil. I know that whatever God does endures for ever; nothing can be added to it, nor anything taken from it; God has done this, so that all should stand in awe before him. That which is, already has been; that which is to be, already is; and God seeks out what has gone by. [1]

The mystery of time—at least within the House—was one I came to share. At the same time each week—after checking and adjusting the accuracy of the timepiece in the chapel (it was, after all, our heart, our spiritual pacemaker)—the Prior would then synchronise all the others in the monastery. At the same time he wound each with a single key, possible by their common manufacture, a task which fell to me among the others as the membership of our order shrank. I wonder if the Trustees found the spare keys. They were appropriately labelled. And I also wonder where those clocks tick now.

Here there is precious little silence to break. I wonder if I would even hear, as I could in the House, the telltale quarter, half, three-quarter and hourly chimes. Sweet music in a way that made the minutes sacred.

So teach us to number our days, that we may apply our hearts unto wisdom. [2]

At times I fail to observe the equanimity I seek. I imagine that I can hear my pulse. Could that even be physically possible? No key can keep the body clock wound up forever. It is a given which, in the fullness of time, will stop.

1. Ecclesiastes 3:10-15
2. Psalm 90:12—here Brother Columba chooses to use the Authorised Version instead of his usual NRSV.

Crisp and Even

Fr Timothy was a master of death. For years CSC's Sacristan, his presence (or evidence of having been in the chapel, despite its emptiness) was authoritative. The Eucharistic vessels sparkled, the small linens were radiant; the altar cloths were starched to within a lift of a matron's arching eyebrow. The atmosphere was calm and beckoning, with just a hint of intimidation.

The effect was heightened by the efforts of others, albeit under his supervision: those who dusted the stalls and other furniture and those, usually novices on their hands and knees, who polished the chapel floor.

At one meeting of Chapter a relatively newly professed member of the community—one, I think, with a background in porterage at a hospital—expressed a desire, almost made a public bid, to take on the Sacristan's duties. Father Abbot was direct: the tasks of the monastery were allocated by him, after taking due account of the skills of the brethren and the needs of the community. That was sufficient to endorse the solidity of Timothy's reign, one that was to remain unbroken under three abbots.

The Sacristan's care for our holy space was never more in

evidence than at funerals. Fr Timothy's immaculate standards somehow seemed to better themselves for a brother's obsequies. The lustre of the floor, the candleware and vessels was put into relief by the simple, unfinished coffins produced by Fr Augustine until arthritis robbed him of his manual skills. Like so many before him who had to relinquish a personal charism, Augustine was initially at a loss to see how he could fulfil his purpose in community without his beloved carpentry. Fr Abbot tackled the issue at Chapter.

'Father Augustine has made his last coffin for the community. That is both a shame and a blessing. It is a shame because we too grieve with Augustine at the loss of his dexterity. But it is a blessing too, in that those of us who have wanted to be buried along with our brethren in the cemetery have often expressed the desire to do so consigned in one of Father Augustine's caskets. Some of us have even thought of putting in an order in advance!' There was a murmur of embarrassed laughter in the Chapter House. 'But, brothers, it is our task not to plan for worldly events—and death, after all, is a very worldly event—but to praise God as we faithfully seek to walk the road, by his grace, to heaven.'

Fr Augustine's simple constructions would be set atop his equally simple and beautifully crafted trestles—I wonder what the Trustees did with all those exquisite pieces? Monastic funerals, as was the case with all ritual at St Candida's, mixed elements of grandeur and simplicity. Fr Abbot, in a black chasuble embroidered with gold thread by one of the founding fathers, would give the homily which encapsulated a eulogy. This would look back—the life of a monk has its antecedents, though pre-profession seemed to some like ancient history— and forward to the hope of eternal life.

Then each member of the community would be called forward to use the aspergillum to sprinkle the coffin. After censing the casket, Fr Abbot would chant the commendation and brothers would hoist it onto their shoulders and carry it out to the cemetery. A simple prayer over the grave, the coffin would be lowered into the hole, and Brother Gardener, transformed by the occasion into Brother Sexton, and a couple of others would fill it in while we sang the final hymn.

As our numbers thinned and our collective strength waned, we found ourselves relying on the services of a local funeral director to provide professional bearers and gravediggers, as well as the simple coffin. Although to us it was still somewhat ornate in comparison with Augustine's work.

When it came to Fr Timothy's turn to take his place in the chapel for his own Requiem, his back story held more surprises than many others.

'Father Timothy left me a brief note,' Fr Abbot began. 'It had been written some years ago, well before his recent physical decline. It said, "At my funeral please do not dwell too much on the events of my life. There is not really much to dwell on. And I am uncomfortable with the idea that you may be speaking about me in chapel while I will be before the throne of Grace, giving an account of my life."

'This, of course, is pure Timothy. Someone who put such effort into appearances—not his own, it has to be admitted, as the monastic habit is hardly for those who want to cut a fashionable dash—not for appearances' sake, but to allow something greater to happen. His meticulous work as sacristan was Biblically inspired—"all things should be done decently and in order".[1] That should come as no surprise to those who remember that Timothy came to Saint Candida's as a novice, stepping down from his duties as Maitre d' at the Connaught in London.

'His attention to detail, his love of work—truly the term "worker-priest" could be used of this, our brother—was for all to see. It not a mark of his pride—and we all carry pride, brothers, for good and ill—to appreciate the gasps of wonder by our Visitor or other episcopal guests when they saw the crispness of the corporal, the sheen of the altar cloth, the sparkle on the brass.

'As we grow together as a community, it is important for us to consider the dual aspects of our calling. We are here to become properly who God wants us to be. We do that as individuals, but more importantly, in our common life. This calls, from time to time, for compromise—something that some of us here are better at accommodating than others.

'Our task is twofold: to be truly who we are, while living with and for those we call brothers. This can seem like a tiny goal, almost miniscule, but I am sure we all know the cost of seeking to walk this path. Father Timothy was among us as a brother. He, as each of us is called to, had to take up his cross daily. In community that cross is both ourselves and each other.

'In my time as Guestmaster I was often taken aback by the rose tinted spectacles through which so many retreatants looked at us. The quiet, the seeming calm, the fellowship of the cloister to them, of course, is exotic. To us it is the grind of daily life.

'Our brother Timothy was not the perfect monk. None of us is, thank God. And surely that is the point. Because the cross we take up daily in community is not just ourselves or others. It is both. It is ourselves in fellowship.

'Let us commend to God our brother Timothy. We remember with fondness his faithfulness, his abilities and skills, and his foibles. As he stands, as he warned me in his note that he would, before the Loving Judge we seek to serve, let us commend him to God's mercy.'

Fr Aidan—nor I for that matter—will not have a monastic funeral. I wonder if The Founder ever foresaw that?

1. 1 Corinthians 14:40

Be Still and Know[1]

Fr Abbot was too unwell to get up today. In fact, he has only been awake for fleeting moments. I spent much of the day in the lounge chair in his room. The radio, no doubt kindly meant by the carers, was not in its usual buzzing, rambling state, perhaps because they had seen me in the room. The silence was welcome.

I took a few turns around the various floors of Care Home. That, along with a lap or two around the block to get some air and sun, is what suffices for exercise for me now. I push away memories of long country walks from and to the monastery. The sound of traffic has replaced the rustling of trees and birdsong.

In the silence—if the rasp that I guessed to be the beginning of Fr Abbot's decline in breathing could be described thus—I recited my morning Office, as well as a period in private meditation and prayers. I essayed some spiritual reading—Julian of Norwich—but even her assurances that all would be well failed to settle me.

It was then I realised that since my accompanying Fr Aidan to London's east end I was routinely in breach of one element of the Rule: that of entering another brother's cell.

There were some exceptions, of course: the Infirmarian in the course of his duties in caring for a brother who was ill; likewise, community members bringing food, or clearing the room on behalf of an incapacitated monk. But these could not be deemed routine or social. A member of CSC kept the spartan accommodation he lived and prayed in clean and clear. It was a discipline that reminded us that we were most free to ponder God in unclutteredness.

And here I was, day after day, in Fr Abbot's cell. His sleeping form, the slight rattle in his chest augmented by the pause between breaths, relief from exhaustion, reminded me of waves on a beach—changeable, yet constant, reassuring in their lolling rhythm.

For a moment I saw myself looking at the breeze coming across from Empire Bay towards the wharf at Bensville. The sheen on the water broke as the wind stirred its surface, a premonition of a stronger blow to follow. And then in my mind, as happens now and then, I was standing on the beach at Macmasters, the sun high at midday, the stillness only broken by that constant roar of the waves. Even then I could be still. Even if I didn't know.[2]

---

1. This section's title is a conscious, though fractured reference to Psalm 46, the complete quote from the tenth verse being, 'Be still and know that I am God'.

2. I suppose my first annotation somewhat gives away the arc of Columba's set-up.

Sins Of The Fathers

I was in the corridor when I heard a newish carer named Luca speaking with Fr Abbot, who has been reluctant to get out of bed. 'Come on, dad, give it a go.' I knocked on the door.

'Can I help?'

'Thanks, but I think we are all right.' He turned to Fr Aidan. 'Aren't we, dad?'

'Please don't call him that.'

'But,' said Luca, 'that's what you call him. I've heard you.' I looked in surprise. 'I was just doing the same.'

'I call him Father. He is my father in God, as he is the abbot of a monastery. Or was. And a priest. Which he still is.'

'I thought he was your father. And that you were, well, a bit standoffish. Formal.'

'Do I look like his son? The age difference is not that great, is it?' To be honest, I don't rightly know how old Fr Abbot is. Luca shrugged. 'So, if you would be so kind, please call him Father. He has been called that for over sixty years.'

'Doesn't look like he wants to get up though, does he?' I agreed that Fr Abbot's rising was becoming something of a challenge.

'Shall I have a go at trying to coax him to get up? Why

don't you come back after you have seen to another resident?'
Father and son. Imagine.

Sacred Plots

I never expected to worry about where my bones would lie. Yet the negotiations between the Trustees and the Robed Buddhists on the sale of the monastery moved the question of my mortal remains from something someone else would deal with to a vexed reality that involved me.

The Community cemetery lies behind the chapel. The generous vision of The Founder was evident in its expanse: he clearly believed all plots in a vast space would eventually be filled by the brethren. In line with his vision, each new grave was marked by a simple, small oak cross—some now in desperate need of repair or replacement—upon which was carved, and in this he was insistent, the name in religion, the years of birth and death, and the date of the monk's profession.

Father Aidan and I are to be buried in this sacred plot. That much is clear. But, given our new steps in our pilgrimage, we will have to return from exile. There is some ache in the realisation that, in the history of our order, we will be the only brothers not to have our funerals in the House chapel.

The Robed Buddhists did not want to use the graveyard, which was a relief, but they did want to claim some of its unused land. Land that was excess to the designated purpose.

While acknowledging and accommodating our desire to be laid to rest there, they resisted the Trustees' suggestion— as I would have done—to open up the graveyard to the monastery's oblates, associates, sympathisers and friends. While recognising people's best intentions in wanting to visit the resting place of those they knew and found influential, it risks—as we found with a number of visitors who sought to incorporate the cemetery as one of the places for meditation on retreat—disturbing the rhythm of the monastery. It is a place useful for contemplation, but one for those within the community. (I should add that this view, like many in the cloistered life, was up for dispute at Chapter.)

Lawyers from both sides came up with a solution. The sticking point was the land had been consecrated. Yet somehow this could be renegotiated. (I am not a lawyer, so I leave interpretation of such matters to experts.) A line was drawn on a map. This would allow eight grave plots to 'square off' the cemetery. Two of these were for the surviving members of the Order—Aidan and me. The other six would be a silent testament to The Founder's hoped-for future and set aside as a place for contemplation. It had always been that. Novices would be sent to spend time there, thinking and praying about the end of this life. It is a practice nearly all of the brethren maintained until they themselves became occupants there.

Access was the other tricky issue. The cemetery was deep into the confines of the monastery's lands. No casual visitors would be able to come, as some did while we remained at St Candida's, to visit the graves of family members or men of spiritual influence. Many of those who returned to the world would come back from time to time to pay their respects, often at the grave of the Novice Master who received, or had to pass on to them, the news that the monastic vocation was not for them.

So, in so far as one can ever know one's future, I know my bones will be in the earth of St Candida's, a place in which I spent much of my life. It will be, much in the same way as Fr Aidan needed to return to Bethnal Green, part of a quest that combined the personal, historical and spiritual. In that, I suppose, there is some kind of resolution.

A Mysterious Meditation

Remember your creator in the days of your youth, before the days of trouble come, and the years draw near when you will say, 'I have no pleasure in them'; before the sun and the light and the moon and the stars are darkened and the clouds return with the rain; on the day when the guards of the house tremble, and the strong men are bent, and the women who grind cease working because they are few, and those who look through the windows see dimly; when the doors on the street are shut, and the sound of the grinding is low, and one rises up at the sound of a bird, and all the daughters of song are brought low; when one is afraid of heights, and terrors are in the road; the almond tree blossoms, the grasshopper drags itself along and desire fails; because all must go to their eternal home, and the mourners will go about the streets; before the silver cord is snapped, and the golden bowl is broken, and the pitcher is broken at the fountain, and the wheel broken at the cistern, and the dust returns to the earth as it was, and the breath returns to God who gave it. Vanity of vanities, says the Teacher; all is vanity.

Besides being wise, the Teacher also taught the people knowledge, weighing and studying and arranging many proverbs. The Teacher sought to find pleasing words, and he wrote words of truth plainly.

The sayings of the wise are like goads, and like nails firmly fixed are the collected sayings that are given by one shepherd. Of anything beyond these, my child, beware. Of making many books there is no end, and much study is a weariness of the flesh.

The end of the matter; all has been heard. Fear God, and keep his commandments; for that is the whole duty of everyone. For God will bring every deed into judgement, including every secret thing, whether good or evil.[1]

1. Br Columba had carefully written out this passage of scripture, Chapter 12, from Ecclesiastes. Clearly he returned to this book repeatedly, as evidenced by the many quotations from it in his musings. That he copied out this passage, the entire chapter—no marks, annotations or commentary— would suggest his effort in doing so was more than a mere passing of time. Perhaps he did it as an aid to memorising it. Though, who is to know? It is, in microcosm, a return to the scribe, repeating the words of scripture, ensuring that it lives for future generations, while meditating on it for oneself.

Changes

What changed where, when? And why? That question—or series of questions—is one that has been put to me by friends, guests, spiritual directors and strangers. What made my move from the world to the monastery so urgent and irrevocable? The truth is that, while it may seem sudden and unchangeable, it was actually gradual and a process that could have been deviated from or terminated at any time, with instigation from the Abbot, Novice Master, the community Chapter and, lest people think the individual has no say in a monastery, by me.

I know my arrival at St Candida's was dramatic—in some people's eyes, at least—but it should be viewed a bit like death. (How pompous my writing can be when I try to make a serious point!) But, having stretched the simile, I shall continue. One of the important things to remember about someone when they die, be they monks or no, is that there is always much more to their lives than the circumstances leading up to their demise.

Father Abbot once said this of Brother Alphege, one of the community, who, in his advancing years, had become spectacularly foul-mouthed and aggressive. In this he eclipsed forty earlier years of gentle, reflective service, especially in the garden and kitchen. His meals, said Father Abbot, were a delight to the eye and the palate. They reflected a deep appreciation of God's gifts to us in nature, and how they can be combined and transformed into food. Alphege celebrated God in horticulture and cuisine. The brothers loved coming to his meals, perhaps too much so. But what was clear in Alphege's cooking was not just skill, which was outstanding, but the love that accompanied it. How could we have known that he had bottled up so much anger and frustration with his brethren? In his active days contemplation provided the counterpoint to work and an outlet for hostility.

Once a guest quizzed me about the seeming placidity of a monk at prayer before the Blessed Sacrament. He was concerned that the stillness was unnatural. I explained that it was the place where reassurance was neither necessarily sought nor extended: it was a place of oneness. Getting to that point was a challenge. Alphege had once built contemplation into all he did, active or passive. When he was unable to do things, a deep reservoir of resentments lavaed to the surface.

I am not really in a place to judge this. Father Abbot used to say that while it was appropriate we spend time daily in self-examination—indeed, it was a vital part of the contemplative vocation—auto-prescription was unhelpful. A spiritual director, or soul friend for those who did not like such hierarchical terms, was necessary. Someone who had an outside view. We learned to make an examen at the end of the day. Its aim is to allow us to understand the events of our lives, to see how close to, or far from, God they have been.[1] By doing this on a daily basis, there is less room for an accumulation of the unmediated good or bad. It is always placed in context. But in the ongoing life of a monk, it was not so much his relationship to himself that matters. It must be tested by his confessor, or in the daily life he has with his brothers. Relying on one's own resources could be deceptive, if not dangerous.

In my own case I moved from an almost rabid need for self-gratification to the discovery of satisfaction within the communal life of the monastery. It was a gradual journey for me, despite the jolting first step. Being found asleep—and hung-over on waking—in the community grounds was a turning point. The cider, the dope, the abusive sex—a thrilling shame always attached itself to the memory of the grunts of pain from Donna as I tried to take her for the last time— culminated in my accompanying a demented monk (no, that should be a monk with dementia) to a home in a puzzlingly busy part of London.

Herein lies—if I may ruminate for a bit—the dilemma: the Christian life is one of living in the now, 'in the moment' as the spiritual directors' fashion had it in the 1980s. To see our spiritual paths in retrospect, or to seek to project them into the future, is to leave the track. Walking is about one step at a time. And the prayerful way is to seek to be in that action. When Jesus warned us that we do not know the hour, he is warning of so much more.[2]

Our lives are really a progression of immediate moments. It is the call of the contemplative to live in that time, while acknowledging its place in eternity. But while we have an awareness of eternity, we cannot be eternally aware. Thus we celebrate being in the present. The challenge of living in Care Home, I have come to realise, is bringing that awareness to a different, fractured context. So many of my co-residents are living in a different time and place—or so it would seem—to the one I am present in.

The centre of the monastery is the chapel. It is both the heart and pacemaker of the community. It is where the brothers come together to regulate their common heartbeat. Prayers, devotions, corporate silence allow the routine busyness of our shared life to flourish.

The care home does not have that intentionality, nor does it have a common place to exercise it. Even the room where the Eucharist is celebrated is used for a variety of purposes—staff training, film afternoons, funeral teas and our mass. What surrounds us is a focus on frailty. The reclusive call for the monastic becomes internal, personal and individual. We daily move from the brethren to the singular. But it is always a journey that has a return ticket. No wonder it is permanently unsettling.

We are all, of course, in need of God's love. But a monastery is a place where that need is openly acknowledged and seeks to build a communal life around it. Here it is inability, rather than need, that takes the upper hand. Some residents cannot wash themselves, move about independently, exercise proper thoughtfulness—not all of us, of course (there are some, like me, who are here for other reasons)—and that creates something of a falsely fragile world. I have no doubt that many residents would not be here if they possessed independence of faculty in mind or body.

One of the local churches, St Matthew's, is often open during the day. I sometimes pop over there for quiet prayer. I have learned to do so at times when I am least likely to encounter anyone there. The Blessed Sacrament is reserved and, because of its setting in a green expanse that is a disused graveyard, the church has a certain charm. The 1960s interior, which contrasts with the Georgian shell, is commanding with an enhanced brutalism—there is a lot of visual art—and shafts of angular light from clear windows that come together to give the space a reflection of the wideness of God's mercy. It is blissfully free of stained glass in the nave. For all that, I can find it difficult to meditate there.

It is not the building that is the problem. It is the journey—and Father Aidan being left alone, the attendant worry about him—along the colourful, smelly, littered, seemingly ever-changing streets with the young professionals, tourists and the fashionable amid the older white and newer Asian residents as they go about their businesses. It all reminds me of how far I have travelled: from my past; from the cloister; from community—to a singular life. The past and present somehow disturb the sought-for now.

I tend to fare better when I am there for Sunday worship. But there are two problems: once again, my concern for Father Aidan, who becomes restive when I leave him for long and, no reflection on them for this, the noise involved in the gathering of St Matthew's parishioners. It would be churlish in the extreme to expect these people who, by and large, seem a mixed, friendly and welcoming lot, to provide a monastic environment. But the chat, the rattling of plastic bags, the children running and calling out seems so foreign to me. What is attractive is the buoyant music and the oases of calm in a lively gathering. It is great to be part of a community, however diffuse, but it remains a long way from the quiet, reflective staple of my spiritual diet. So I tend to arrive as close as possible to the ringing of the bell which signals the commencement of the first hymn.

Many people, priests among them, would admit on retreat that they felt either confronted or comforted by the monastic style of worship. For some it allows an essence, a kind of homeopathic release in miniature, of the spiritual quest. For others, for whom emotion and sensation are the leading stimuli—such people often refer to themselves as 'charismatic' but they are, God forgive me, often seemingly self-obsessed and dull—St Candida's presented a dry monotony, lacking excitement. That is probably unfair to all our visitors.

So I find myself on the receiving end of parochial religion. The parish model is obviously absorbing for the clergy and many members of the church but the constant running about, trying to alternately enthuse or placate, seemed to give little time for prolonged adoration. Watching the priests spread themselves about over coffee was deeply affecting. I have taken to leaving pretty sharply after the end of the service.

I never really get a chance to speak to Father Scully about this. He is efficient, breezing into Care Home, bring energy and (false?) cheer, says the mass with a combination of focus and vigour, but has an air of needing to rush on, if not to something better, to something else. He combines two parts of the law of inertia—he does not strike me as a body that tends to remain at rest.

So much of monastic life, I have come to realise now that I have left the cloister, was about settlement. For me, and I suppose for many of my brothers, that was physical, captured in the grounds and buildings of St Candida's. Yet the buildings, like we who lived in them, are transitory. Successive abbots would stress that in Chapter. Work was prayer and the maintenance of the gifts of the monastery we held in trust had only one end—to praise God.

I suppose parish life is another form of that vocation. The faithful of St Matthew's gather joyfully and noisily, even if sometimes painfully so to me. At the core is a beautiful building that tells a fascinating history. For me its pleasures unfold in solitary visits—its expanse, the light cascading on the parquet floors, the verdancy of the surrounding grounds which are home to the remains of eighty thousand people.

Yet such visits are necessarily brief and rare. I do not like to leave Father Aidan for too long. If the surroundings of Care Home disorient me, a relatively resilient and aware individual, they can overwhelm Father Abbot. He has not only lost the beating heart of the chapel, the torso of the monastery, the limbs of the gardens and grounds, he has, it has to be admitted, slipped from possession of his mind. Watching his distress has been the biggest cross I have had to bear.

1. The Examen is a spiritual practice, much as Columba describes it, first formulated by St Ignatius of Loyola, founder of the Jesuits.

2. 'But about that day or hour no one knows, neither the angels in heaven, nor the Son, but only the Father. Beware, keep alert; for you do not know when the time will come.' (Mark 13:32-33)

EDITOR'S NOTE

It is a startling, and not always a comforting, awareness that flows from an assessment of one's work and style. I have often expressed the opinion that priests could benefit from the equivalent of a schools' inspector, someone who can provide a form of external assessment. Brother Columba's comments certainly provided that. I wonder what grade he would have given me?

I have also often told colleagues that I draw delight from my visits to Care Home. Watching people reconnect, a momentary repair of damaged memories, providing some line to a world beyond the home, being with the residents as Christ makes himself present in our midst in the sacrament—these I have always counted as great stimuli for maintaining such work.

Some of Br Columba's comments draw me up. The bouncy jollity, the seeming rushing in and out— 'I know you're busy, Father'— 'energy', '(false?) cheer', and 'vigour'. Seeing the assessment in Columba's own hand poses many questions: am I playing to the gallery? Is the liturgy some kind of armour I put on to avoid deeper engagement with people? Is ministry bluff, a mere delivery of set pieces delivered at regular times, avoiding a deeper connection with those I am called to serve?

I do draw some solace from his comments not about me, but the church. Striving to keep it open, with the inevitable drawbacks of anti-social activity, is worth it. The number of people who take refuge, finding a quiet space, lighting candles, or even just sitting, are a testament to the value of taking the risk. As I get older myself, I find time alone in prayer before God more enlivening than much of the wider church's agenda.

The spectre of growth has stalked me for over twenty years. It seems, listening to bishops' rattling their sabres on the subject from time to time, that some may think we relish failure. Failure, perhaps congenitally, has been with me for much of my life. But with God there is no failure. We grow in grace toward acceptance, as I have seen people grow in grace as they move towards the grave.

Watching communities shrink is painful. But the risk is to dismiss or devalue, as Columba is on the verge of doing in relation to his own brotherhood, the faithful but now unfashionable witness of those who have gone before us. So much of the fruitfulness agenda is marked by sociology rather than theology, a drum I seem to bang at the risk of breaking its skin.

Bethnal Green is ample evidence of the importance of marketing and change. When I arrived here all the pubs were pitching for the same diminishing market with the same tired strategies—football, karaoke, tribute acts. The transformation of pubs here has recognised incomers as their lifeblood and they have adapted, offering good food, a hip ambiance, craft beers. It is one of the few parts of the country where pubs are reopening.

No doubt the moves at new-style churches are the same. They seem to plug into the zeitgeist (even if the music is retroschmaltz) and they do the job. The challenge is for people like me, who have moved from being the bright eyed boy to boring old fart, is where to go? The sad realisation is that St Matthew's is like St Candida's, and I am Brother Columba.

Office Work—1

One morning, sitting with Father Aidan, he broke from his usual distracted silence.

'Have we done the morning office, Brother?'

I had done mine privily in his room earlier. I usually join him in case he wants to pray but most mornings he is content to sit in his chair, office book unopened. At first I would recite the office for him but he did not seem to take notice, so I had taken to reading it quietly, hoping the silence in which I read it would suffice for the prayers on the page. Words read aloud had sometimes led to an assembly of distracting thoughts as Aidan made connections that had coherence for himself alone.

'It is the feast of Saint Bartholomew, is it not?'

'It is, Father.'

'I do not recall our having said the Quicunque Vult at Morning Prayer.'

I looked at him blankly.

'The Quicunque Vult, more popularly, though incorrectly, known as the Athanasian Creed. It is recited on the majority of the Apostles' feast days. I don't recall this happening.'

Father Abbot then set out to right whatever liturgical oversight he had determined by launching into the prayer or lecture, 'Which Faith except every one do keep whole and undefiled: without doubt he shall perish everlastingly.' One, three, Almighty, incomprehensible, as is aforesaid—the entire list of qualities rightly to be held. He then sat in contented silence until:

'Oh, no. That was before the monastery wasn't it? The BCP. Ah, yes. Still, I am sure Saint Bartholomew wouldn't mind.'

What led to this connection? Living in a building where many of the residents have dementia is properly unnerving. Their mysterious thought processes can often derail one's own. The shouted patronisation of some of the staff and visitors—is it some kind of defence mechanism?—can make it worse. Sometimes, when a new member of staff joins, I find myself among the ranks of the receiving end of these raised voices. Or maybe it is just an assumption that the would-be hearer is deaf.

Sometimes I choose to play along, assuming the incapacities being projected on me. I regret doing so almost immediately. Being of sound mind cuts little grass here. The really clear headed people, I have found, tend not to socialise, even with each other. They (we?) tend to retreat into their rooms. One has no television or radio, as I do. (Father Aidan has a radio, sometimes tuned, no doubt through the best motives of one of the staff, to a Christian radio station. It is gall to me, so I turn it off.) Yet cutting oneself off only leads to a deeper isolation.

Prayer is the cornerstone.[1]

---

1. It would appear Columba left off his thoughts here. I find this enticing. Was he interrupted? Did the potentially vast subject daunt him? Had he

nothing to say? I doubt it; he must have had so much experience to draw on. Or is it, as St Teresa of Avila tells us, pure gift in a depth of quiet. As Hamlet, said, 'The rest is silence'. Maybe that is what Columba was pointing to. Though another jotting, which I have placed to follow this one, may give us an insight into his reticence.

Office Work—2

There is perhaps an understandable assumption that monks, by virtue of their lifestyle and spiritual practices, are models of perfection. I suppose there are examples of that. Reading the greats like Teresa of Avila[1] or Bernard of Clairvaux points in that direction. But accounts of their lives—at least, those that do not tilt towards hagiography—show these luminaries were, for the most part, very earthen vessels indeed.

In CSC there were certainly some luminaries: Alphonse, whose learning was masked by a deep simplicity: never flustered, never put out by the menial or the manual tasks, but a man of profound wisdom; someone whose time in the chapel seemed to be pure repose. If one ventured in there for personal meditation and Alphonse was in his stall, prayer always seemed assured and calm. His death provoked outbursts of pettiness and squabbles—such was the corporate placidity that flowed from his presence.

It should not—indeed, it did not—rely on individuals. The corporate discipline existed to allow, if not immediately, but in time, disruption. A renewed sense of identity would emerge: changed, seeking to reflect the new now of community life. That was, as successive abbots would remind us, the purpose of monastic life—to live in the present.

So many of these reflections, penned as I fill in time here in Care Home, seem to drift off—dwelling on or recollecting lost time. Though no time is really 'lost'; it passes. Drifting off, our Novice Master would warn us neophytes, was a way of avoiding the present. So much of present life for my fellow residents—I cannot call it a community—seems to be spending, filling (dare I say wasting?) time until the call that is both universal and unique in its circumstances.

1. St Teresa penned *The Way of Perfection*.

What I am saying, brothers and sisters, is this: flesh and blood cannot inherit the kingdom of God, nor does the perishable inherit the imperishable. Listen, I will tell you a mystery! We will not all die, but we will all be changed, in a moment, in the twinkling of an eye, at the last trumpet. For the trumpet will sound, and the dead will be raised imperishable, and we will be changed. For this perishable body must put on imperishability, and this mortal body must put on immortality. When this perishable body puts on imperishability, and this mortal body puts on immortality, then the saying that is written will be fulfilled:

'Death has been swallowed up in victory.'

'Where, O death, is your victory?

'Where, O death, is your sting?'

The sting of death is sin, and the power of sin is the law. But thanks be to God, who gives us the victory through our Lord Jesus Christ.

Therefore, my beloved, be steadfast, immovable, always excelling in the work of the Lord, because you know that in the Lord your labour is not in vain.[1]

---

1. 1 Corinthians 15:50-58 — another random quotation from the Bible, handwritten by Columba, with no key as to what prompted him to do so.

Dropping Stitches

One afternoon I joined a couple of women in the lounge on the first floor. The young one—though that should be a comparative, as she was far from the first flush of youth, her companion edging or toppling over the age of 90—sat calmly as her hands dealt deftly with needles and wool. I recognised the old lady, always turned out in smart, pressed clothes of neutral colours, as a fellow resident, one with whom I had never had a conversation.

I asked if I could sit down. The woman looked up from her knitting, nodded vigorously and said, 'Of course. We would be glad of the company. Wouldn't we, Mum?' The old lady seemingly ignored her. I took my seat. I mentioned not a word had passed between her mother and myself.

'Oh, I wouldn't take that personally,' she said. 'I can't remember when Mum last spoke to me.' She turned and smiled at her mother. 'What was it? Ten years ago?'

A slow turning of the head. There was a mixture of deadness and interest in the older woman's eyes. No raising of the eyebrows, no tilting of the head, the rotation having been sufficient acknowledgement that she had been mentioned.

'You did well,' said the daughter as her mother turned

her head away. 'It used to drive me nuts. I would come in and witter on, reporting family news, commenting on this and that—the news, the weather, politics, even sport—and get nothing. My sister can't handle it. She comes in once a week like me. That's our agreement. She does Saturday and I come on Tuesdays. But I know fifteen minutes is about her limit. We see each other regularly. She can't handle the silence. She can't take the fact—is it a fact? —that Mum does not seem to even know who we are and shows no interest in what we do.'

I ventured to comment, 'Maybe she's had enough? Pardon me,' I said, intending to include both of them.

'We all have, to be honest. God knows why she is dragging it out.' She looked at me. 'Sorry. I suppose I shouldn't have said that. You being a priest and all.'

'I'm not a priest.' There followed a brief, but ultimately futile, attempt to explain the difference between lay and ordained members of a male religious community.

All the while the woman's fingers moved in small arcs, sometimes picking up the string of wool with a lift and fall of the needles which, every now and then, gave an occasional click. She saw I was watching.

'It helps pass the time. As I said, I come in every week. I come just after lunch and sit with Mum till tea time. She never liked television. The carers will turn it on in her room. My sister bought it for her. They mean well, I suppose. But she was always proper. Liked us to sit in the front room and talk. Social-like.' She gave a slight laugh. 'Talk about talk! Her! But she was a brilliant knitter. Taught me. But never picks up the needles now.'

I asked her what she was working on.

'It changes. I used to do a lot of baby clothes. But people

don't seem to like that kind of thing now. They like labels, fashion. For a baby! Sometimes jumpers, they can be fun. But you have to have someone who wants them. I have one grandson who likes a new one now and then. Socks. Now they are a challenge.'

She explained the techniques of using four open ended shorter needles—she liked to use bamboo because they had a kind of holding traction that metal and plastic did not—and the variegated colours in sock wool that formed a surprisingly coherent pattern. She talked of the concentration required to turn a heel and the delight she felt in completing a toe.

'And then you have to do it all over again for the second sock. But it didn't seem right. You can't really do anything else when you're knitting a sock. Like this, I couldn't be talking to you right now. You have to concentrate.' She paused to look at her handiwork. 'This is a very simple job. Different colours. Short ends of balls of wool. I knit them up into squares, then sew them together into a rug or throw. There's a nun who collects them—maybe you know her, Sister Julia?—and they send them off to refugee camps. Feel like I am doing a bit of good while visiting Mum.' Who, all the while, had sat staring into what Peter Porter had described as 'crowded emptiness'.[1]

I excused myself not long after. The easy social chatter, in which the knitting lady was clearly adept and grateful for a listener, reminded me—did I need reminders?—of the buzzing noises around me and how far I had travelled from the silences of St Candida's.

It is not that I am socially withdrawn. A substantial part of my life has been spent in regulated order. And silence was one of the threads knitted into the garment of daily living. As the Novice Master once said, 'Silence should be neither a denial nor a drudgery. If it feels like either, it is probably not your vocation to be in a place like this. This is not a condemning judgment, merely a realisation that we all have different gifts and discomfort may be a sign that you may not be called to the cloister. If not denial or drudgery, what is it? Discipline. The regulations, the Rule, are there for us to be free in. If it does not work for you, God may well be calling you to something else.'

I went to my room. After a period of reading, I popped in to check on Fr Aidan. He was in bed, sleeping. I noticed a loose thread on his habit which was hanging on a hook on the wall. This brought to mind the interconnectedness of monastery life; of how much we depended on others.

I thought of Fr Ambrose, a tailor in the world, who found himself general overseer of fabric—in the sense of cloth, not buildings and the like—in CSC. He was the go-to monk for tutoring in how to repair or maintain your habit. On occasion he would do the work himself, saying it would be quicker for him to make good the defect than to explain the technique and supervise the process. The onset of arthritis frustrated not only him, but other members of the community who now could no longer rely on Fr Ambrose's skills. Oddly, his incapacity with the needle liberated him. He took to sitting in chapel for prolonged periods. Once, at recreation, I asked him how he could spend so long in prayer.

'Making up for lost time, brother. Making up for lost time.'

From nowhere came a recollection from school at Woy Woy. One boy—I see his face, yet grasp to recall a name—wore a hand-knitted pullover. It was in the colour of the school uniform, even sporting the thin double stripes of yellow on the neckline and cuffs. The lad was looked down on, pitied, bullied even, because he stood out from the rest of us, turned out in machined knitwear. His jumper we thought a badge of poverty.

I realise now that the pullover was the result of labour, hours of concentrated work to produce a thing of beauty. For a moment I saw in a mirage of diversity, like Hopkins's song to working man's kit.[2] I let my fancy take wing. I saw the mother of the boy—I don't think I had ever seen her, which is not a surprise given I can't recall his name—lacing each loop over the clicking needles, her fingers weaving her affection into the wool, turning out more than a garment, but a token of love.

1. Peter Porter was an Australian-born poet. The reference comes from his poem *Phar Lap in the Melbourne Museum*. Phar Lap was a famous racehorse.
2. Columba is referring to *Pied Beauty* by Gerard Manley Hopkins:
Glory be to God for dappled things—
   For skies of couple-colour as a brinded cow;
     For rose-moles all in stipple upon trout that swim;
Fresh-firecoal chestnut-falls; finches' wings;
   Landscape plotted and pieced—fold, fallow, and plough;
     And áll trádes, their gear and tackle and trim.
All things counter, original, spare, strange;
   Whatever is fickle, freckled (who knows how?)
     With swift, slow; sweet, sour; adazzle, dim;
He fathers-forth whose beauty is past change:
Praise him.

The Place of No Return

For some reason today Fr Scully stayed on after the mass. The carers were signally efficient in gathering up the residents at the conclusion of the service to take them to their respective dining rooms. For all that, as one of them noted to me as she satisfied herself that all who required assistance had been rendered it, there was a quarter of an hour to wait before the meal. She also assured me that Father Abbot was quite content.

Fr Scully had flopped into the chair next to me. He had closed his eyes and sat in silence for some minutes. When he eventually opened his eyes again, I asked, 'Tired?'

'Not really, Brother. Just taking advantage of a few minutes quiet. Some mornings it is just one thing after another without a break. And the next day there will be precious little to do. It would be great if you could somehow level it out to be tackled evenly each day.'

'You looked so far away for a minute there,' I said.

'Yes. A short prayer and a visualisation. I find that usually does the trick.'

'Do you go anywhere in particular?' I asked.

'What, in my head?'

'Yes.'

'Well,' he said, 'I don't know why but I often find myself lying on a towel on a sunny day at Macmasters Beach. That's on the Central Coast of New South Wales. My parents moved there. As to my image, it's funny, I can even put a year to it by the swimmers I'm wearing. The sound of the surf, the warmth of the sun on my body, the relative seclusion of the place…' He laughed. 'I was on my own that day for some reason. Funny, I haven't been there in years.'

What were the chances of his mentioning Macmasters Beach? I could have told him about Bensville, my parents, my journey here. But there seemed little point. After all, I have been scribbling away about those things. I thought it best to keep the lid on. What could be served in talking about it now? So we sat in silence for a while. I thought maybe he would understand if I left these papers for him when—if—I leave Care Home.

'I used to go back— to Australia— every couple of years. To see my parents when they were alive, God rest their souls. I still have a sister there.'

Somehow this led to an offer for him to show me some pictures. Not his own, thank heavens, but ones on the internet. He told me you could just put 'Bensville' into a search engine and a host of images come up. It is, he said, a gift to the lazy traveller.

I thanked him for the offer. But, as I told him, they would mean nothing to me. I did not tell him I would simply compare it to what I remember. Which, in itself, is harmless enough. But it is not really about now. And that is the call of faith. To live now. In the presence of God. Now. Lord knows what sort of memories I would dredge up if I saw the Brisbane Water again.

CAT AND MOUSE

I had an erection today. It came quite out of the blue, unbidden by thought or occasion—there was no-one about who could have been thought to embody the pulchritude that gave rise to the private part of my person.

I was startled, much as I was when I encountered a mouse in the guests' kitchen, or a large spider as I cleaned a room in the Guest Wing. In both cases it was a confrontation with a creature that was simply out of place. And in both cases I knew what to do. For the mouse I would either lay a trap or borrow Brother Kitchen's cat. The very presence of a feline seemed to do the trick. But she was such a good mouser that capture and despatch was both rapid and effective.

With a spider, a large glass from the kitchen would hold the arachnid in what looked like an inverted fishbowl while I got my special postcard—one I reserved solely for this purpose—from the Guestmaster's drawer, sliced it over the mouth of the glass, usually incensing the creature whose apparent fangs were bared to alert the reluctant predator—me—that no good would come of the encounter. I would then carry the glass, holding the card to it, and, having reached a door or window, fling the creature to the outside world. Though once one ran back with such speed that it crossed the threshold before I did. It was a couple of days before we renewed our acquaintance and I placed the animal at a greater remove.

But today's guest in my body—once both the centre of my consciousness and drive—stayed for a few minutes and seeped away. Leaving me to ponder just that: when did I lose the drive for sex and become content with contentment?

THE DYING VIGIL

It is surprising how sustaining living among people with dementia can be. At first there is a sympathy mixed with anger, tempered by the clichéd realisation that 'it's all right' for those with the disease—they are unaware, or so we are told, of their condition so the amusing, fractious, alarming and confronting symptoms do not matter. For them the ship is sailing as normal.

In the monastery there was a profound element of distraction: the brothers whose powers were beginning to evaporate initially seemed ashamed that their behaviour had disrupted the ordered agenda of community living. A monk is always seeking to be, but not attract attention to, himself. I have written elsewhere that this is a veneer: the routine discipline of daily life, while lived out in a pattern, is one of infinite variety for both individual and community.

In the care home the outrageous becomes predictable. There is a woman who screams for much of the day—and through the night if her medication is not precisely monitored—in what, on first hearing, raises the deepest alarm. Someone is being attacked, murdered. It was under this apprehension, mistaken as it turned out, that I rushed to her room, only to find her alone, with a cup of tea in her plastic beaker with its straw-like spout on the sliding table in front of her. As soon as she saw me she was overcome by calm.

'Where's Margaret?' she asked. I had no idea who Margaret was. I came to learn it was her elder sister who had lived with her in a council flat that had been raised out of the ruins of the Blitzed east end. Both women had lost fiancés in a battle in the Japanese theatre of the war. Margaret had died some ten years earlier.

The sisters were local legends. United in a narrative of common grief, they soldiered through the recovering East End as machinists in the rag trade, school dinner ladies at the same establishment and, for a while, cleaners of the same City offices. Margaret, so long the bookend to her isolation and sadness, had toppled, allowing nothing but singular horrors of life to flow in. And hence the scream.

Care Home's corridors rang out during the day with a symphony of alarm calls. The almost incessant bleeping of strategically placed wall units through the facility meant the staff were never far from learning which room—a number would be displayed on the beeping box—and respond, or as it happened sometimes, not.

Like all activities, there were serial offenders in pressing the button or pulling the cord that led to the aural assaults. At first newly inducted staff would run to the panel and rush to visit the summoner. But in time response became one that was slotted into other duties—being with fragile people requires care and assistance and leaving someone may render them vulnerable—so it can prove problematic. You can't leave someone in the bath to investigate who had instigated the alarm.

In an almost mystical development, some of the carers had

an innate sense of an emergency, or a summons from someone not numbered among Louis Renault's 'usual suspects'.[1] There was the odd occasion—staff distracted, otherwise engaged, involved in a delicate situation—when a resident in a real emergency had to wait but this was, thankfully, very rare.

Life among the unpredictable strangely has its patterns and the disordered clash of alternating realities, for those of us inhabiting a different world and time in the same space, can be frustrating and entertaining. In Father Aidan's mind I have become a range of members of CSC, some whom even he would not have met face to face. One afternoon I came into his room to find Father Abbot holding a photograph—Lord knows where he had obtained it—of The Founder standing among the foundations of the first chapel of the monastery. He then informed me, in extraordinary detail, of the challenges of securing the site in Dorset.

It had long been claimed—and subsequent archaeological digs had confirmed—that there had been a small monastery on the land that was to become the site of the Community of Saint Candida. It had been a mixed community of women and men, its first leader an Abbess. The experiment apparently failed because of the openness of the vision. Not only did the monks and nuns pray together, but they sought to live a full daily life as brothers and sisters. The salacious would no doubt suggest some kind of grubby conspiracy, à la Matthew Lewis[2], but it is more likely to have been a more sedate and humane failure. Two brothers and two sisters fell in love, became two couples and, having left the community to set up as marrieds in the nearby village, embarked on family life. The effect on the nascent monastery was terminal.

The demise of the spiritual aspirations of this community

was pursued by its physical obliteration. Long dead before the rampages of the rapacious Henry VIII and the later Vandal-in-Chief Oliver Cromwell, locals used the ruins of the community buildings as a pre-cut quarry, so much so that a number of academic explorations have claimed that holy stones can be found in constructions as diverse as the village pub, defunct post office, schoolhouse and in various dry stone walls throughout the county.

Fr Abbot spoke to The Founder—that is, to me, whom he imagined to be The Founder—and asked if he had foreseen the decay and demise of the project he had worked so hard to foster. Here I faced the perennial dilemma of dealing with the demented. Did I attempt to disabuse Fr Aidan of his assumption as to my persona, telling him that I was no more than Brother Columba, unfit to untie the thong of the sandal of The Founder? Should I ignore it? Or did I play along? This is fraught with danger. Fr Aidan's bouts of clarity drew on his prodigious brain and experience, and any such role play was bound to end unhappily as I grasped to respond to technical and historical enquiry.

What I chose was ultimately a path of cowardice and responsibility. I asked him if he wanted a cup of tea. He responded in the affirmative. I popped off to the kitchen to which I had been given, by virtue of my relatively clear mind, more or less free access, and brewed us both a cup. On my return I was amazed to see that Fr Abbot had got out of his clothes—they were in a pile on the floor—and had got into bed. This show of initiative was worrying. Fr Aidan had long relied on the agency of carers to dress and undress, as well as getting out of and into bed. Yet here he was tucked up. I later remarked on this to one of the night staff who registered little surprise; good habits, just as much as the bad, she said, came to the unexpected fore.

It being near the hour of Compline I suggested, with little real expectation of enthusiasm, that we do the office together. Fr Aidan readily assented and I took up his rarely used office book and attempted to give it to him. He waved it away.

'Gracious, no, Brother. If a monk does not know Compline after all the years we've been professed, what is to become of us?'

I asked if he minded that I, then, might resort to the use of his prayer book, saving me the journey to my adjoining room.

'Not at all, Brother.'

He then, for the first time in our residence at Care Home, took the role of officiant. I responded to his deftly clipped versicles, joined his singing of Before the Ending of the Day, Save us O Lord and the Nunc Dimittis (for which he switched to the BCP 1662 Evensong version), and gave his abbatial blessing at the conclusion. All of which was done in a manner that nobly reflected his authority gained from a lifetime in the cloister.

No sooner had he pronounced the blessing than his eyes closed and was asleep. I folded his clothes, put them on the now vacated chair, put his office book on the prie-dieu and took the empty cups back to the kitchen where I had the conversation with the carer I mentioned earlier. I returned to my room, took off my habit and got into bed.

Morning in a care home, like the rest of the day, is a mixture of the predictable and unexpected events. Some residents refuse to rise; some need especial attentions dealing with unwelcome deposits overnight; others seek to regiment a routine for themselves that somehow mirrors the beginning of the day when they lived in places they called their own.

I had taken to saying a shorter morning office on rising. I did this at my prayer desk after taking advantage of the en-suite bathroom where I showered before donning my habit and scapular. I would then pop in to see Fr Aidan where I offered, if he wanted—he usually did not—to say the longer office. I would read aloud a reflective non-scriptural passage appointed for the day, which he seemed to welcome.

This morning followed its customary routine: I showered, dressed, took to my knees to pray. Then, recognising the gift of Fr Aidan's clarity at bedtime, I gave thanks to God for a glimmer of the towering figure Fr Abbot had been—prayerful, incisive, commanding, a natural administrator and leader, but always a wise priest. I usually held off intercessions and other prayers of the office for that, if were to happen, I conducted with my fellow monk in exile. If he did not, I found time during the morning to do this work.

So, after my mixture of enhanced routine, I knocked on the door of the adjoining room. Gaining no response was no surprise—I was often greeted with silence. I pushed back the door and went in. Fr Aidan was in his bed. He was stone dead.

1. Br Columba is referring to the film *Casablanca*.

2. Author of the novel, *The Monk*.

Man is like a thing of nought: his time passeth like a shadow.[1]

1. Psalm 144:4. Columba is quoting from the Coverdale Psalter, used in the Book of Common Prayer, 1662. There is nothing to suggest why this quotation was put on the scrap of paper on which it appears.

PRECIOUS MOMENTS

Being with the dead is a precious gift. I am not suggesting anything morbid or romantic here—I expect those who work in mortuaries and funeral directors have some kind of sustaining drive, be it prayer, cynicism or even gallows humour—but there is a sacred confrontation: one witnesses a departure (there is no doubt a body becomes a mere husk of something once animate) and a responsibility is laid on such witness.

In the monastery the death of a brother was celebrated: not quite with a party, but due observance. The laying out was usually the task of the Infirmarian, so much did we see the link between the fragility of life and acceptance of death as part of it. We were fortunate to have a former doctor and nurse in that role during different times of my life at Saint Candida's, and then Father Abbot and the Sacristan would oversee the ritual.

There was a beautiful pattern to this. Laid out in one of Fr Augustine's simple coffins, the deceased brother would lie in chapel where a prayer vigil was maintained by members of the community. Work was expected to continue as normal. As Fr Abbot would remind us, our departed brother was still alive, but not present to us here; he was doing the work now required of him, and so we should do ours.

A Requiem Mass would follow the next day—assuming no other legal or civic investigations were required—and the priests and brothers would follow the coffin to the monastery cemetery where the monk would be laid to rest. It was all simple, solemn yet, in a strange way, joyful. Wine would be served with the lunch that followed the ceremony.

Fr Aidan's death in Care Home presented the community— me—with the task of dealing with death without such a monastic framework. Father Abbot was dead—there was no question of it. And there was no point in panicking or raising an alarm.

I popped next door to my room, collected my office book and returned to Fr Aidan's room. I recited the office for the dead and then said Morning Prayer. It was then I sought out one of the carers. It was just approaching handover time at the change of shifts. I knew this was potentially tricky: the night staff would be keen to leave and those coming on for morning duties had plenty to do, let alone deal with the death of one of the residents.

Such misgivings were as unfair to the staff as they were unfounded. After all, death in a care home is a part of life there as much as it was as in a monastery. The woman I had spoken with in the kitchen during the night was in the dining room. I told her what had occurred and she reacted with sympathetic and unhurried concern. A Christian herself, she asked me if we should pray. I told her I had already said the office for the dead. The look on her face—she was a Pentecostalist— informed me these words meant nothing to her. So we went to Fr Aidan's room and she led me in what she said was going to be a short prayer. I suppose it was to her, but it did seem to go on for a long time.[1]

'You should call a priest,' she said. 'Isn't that what you do? Do you have a number? We should leave things as they are and let the office know when they arrive in a while.'

I gave the woman Fr Scully's number and I went with her to a phone. She dialled the number and, when it was ringing, handed me the handset. Fr Scully answered. I told him the news.

'I'll be right over.'

I waited with Fr Abbot's body until I heard the telltale buzz that alerted staff someone was at the front door—you learn to distinguish each of the clarion calls in various panels of the home's corridors. I went downstairs and let the priest in.

Fr Scully asked when Fr Aidan had died and I recounted the events of the evening and following morning. When we got to the room, Fr Scully slipped over his head a thin purple stole taken from a black leather holder, which also contained a small silver sprinkler, with a screw top in the shape of a cross. He undid the top and sprayed the room as he began to read from a small brown covered prayer book.

'Rest eternal grant unto him, O Lord…' he began.

I joined in the response, 'and let light perpetual shine upon him.'

There followed the De Profundis, Psalm 130, 'Out of the depths I cry to you, O Lord…' A mixture of prayers followed: some scripted; some *ex tempore*. At one point I heard myself asked if I wanted to say something. I shook my head, then told Fr Scully I had already prayed the Community Office for the departed. He nodded, then began the Lord's Prayer, followed by a prayer of commendation. The service ended as it opened, praying for eternal rest for my now departed brother.

'Would you like a cup of tea?' It was Fr Scully. I did.

We went to the kitchen, made a cup each, then adjourned to the sitting room where the weekly Eucharist was celebrated. I recall little of the conversation. It is possible we sat in silence. There did not seem anything to say. The priest had conducted his duties decently and in order.

For a brief moment I experienced an emotion similar to that I had after the death of my parents in the car crash. I was an orphan again. I was the last of my clan. All that could be said about the Community of Saint Candida, as with my family, was in the past. The rest was silence.

1. The staff member asked me to anonymise her if Brother Columba's writings were ever made public. She said she was worried she could face disciplinary action for having prayed over a resident.

Obituary

Fr Aidan of the Community of Saint Candida, who died last week in a care home in East London, was for many the archetypal Anglo-Catholic intellectual.

Born Cyril Rochdale, he was the only child to Bert and Doris, who ran a stall in Cheshire Street, off the famous Brick Lane market. Evacuated during the war to Suffolk, it was there he learned of the death of his parents, who were killed in a bombing raid, from Captain and Mrs Everton, in whose care he had been lodged. The young Cyril remained in the care of the Evertons, who formally adopted him, though he retained his parents' surname.

An excellent scholar at grammar school, he won a place at New College, Oxford, which he took up after his National Service. His academic prowess, for which he gained a double first from Oxford, led to an early career as tutor, lecturer and author, specialising in Recusant Roman Catholicism.

He was tipped for professorial status but upended expectations by joining the relatively obscure and remote order of the Community of St Candida in rural Dorset. After his novitiate he was encouraged by the Abbot to maintain his academic links while, at the same time, living within the daily routine of the monastery. It was the same Abbot who discerned a priestly vocation in him. He was ordained by the Visitor to the Order as both deacon and priest.

Numerous students consulted Fr Aidan, as he now was, in person or by letter, to which he responded in his signature copperplate handwriting. He never took to technology—not even a typewriter—which probably accounted for his shrinking presence in academe. His reviews in this journal and other publications were examples of the best in the genre—insightful, critical and always concise. He had the gift of understanding the complex and reflecting on it simply. For all that his views, both private and public, seemed free of any 'party politics' or controversies that have arisen within the Church of England.

Fr Aidan served in many posts of the monastic 'hierarchy'—Prior, Novice Master, Librarian and, for a short time (much to the relief of his brethren) in charge of the kitchen. He was elected Abbot in his fifties, serving as the spiritual head of the monastery for 13 years.

He was a much sought after retreat conductor, quiet day leader, spiritual director and confessor by priests and laymen alike. His kind, sympathetic nature was combined with a keen eye for people's talents. No less than three bishops found their initial vocation through his nurture.

As the numbers of monks dwindled, Fr Aidan reluctantly found himself Abbot once again. A peculiarity of CSC is that only a priest could serve in the abbatial role. In this post he oversaw the personally painful but necessary sale of the monastic buildings and the transfer of its assets to a Trust that serves to look after the remaining member of the community and other objectives that seek to further prayerful reflection in the Church of England.

As his physical and mental faculties began to diminish, the Trustees acceded to his wish to return to East London where he began life, a development no-one had foreseen. He made the move with Brother Columba, who is now the last remaining member of CSC.[1]

1. The obituary appeared in the Church Times. It was credited to the Chair of Trustees.

The Court of Earls

I keep avoiding—at least in writing—the collision of values that led to my coming to Saint Candida's. London life took on an increasingly dissolute quality—crammed flats, cases of beer drunk, parties interrupted by the necessity to find time and ways to pay for them. Who knew there were so many Australians who had British ancestry, who were travelling in Europe in the company of others from a similar background?

We shared ourselves around. There seemed an acceptance that all involved were prepared to share homes, meals, beds and bodies with each other. Somehow relationships, however transitory, were formed. We revelled in the public aspect of private matters. Having sex in a room with others doing similarly became normal. Apologies were not offered for interrupting. Indeed, the thought of interruption did not seem to occur to the participants.

I bought a redundant Kombi off a man whose time was up—he was going back to Adelaide to 'get on with life', as though the years he had passed here were no more than a notch on his belt—and had to get rid of the hardware. Like him, and countless others before him, I proceeded to fill the vehicle with fellow travellers of indeterminate desire for each other and length of journey. It seemed that any outgoing tide of people or interest would be met by one that came the other way.

The transaction took place outside Australia House in the Strand. The vendors were all at the end of their current venture and wanted a bit of cash so they could move on to the next chapter of their book of life. This might be on land, sea or in the air. Paperwork for cars seemed historical, like oral history, an unbroken but hazy relationship that stretched back to original sources. The advice was simple: if you were stopped, say you had borrowed the van; it was easier that way.

There were always complications. Those of us in the vehicle would rotate liaisons, affections and jealousies. This led to sometimes sudden departures at motorway services, towns and villages along the way.

We ended up at the Isle of Wight Festival. Apparently I saw Jimi Hendrix. I would like to claim this with certitude, but that part of the story is too befuddled in my mind. I say apparently because my memories of that part of my journey are covered in haze, but not purple or any other colour for that matter. The music, the people, the booze, the dope just seemed to flow in a strange river. The escape was obviously individual. Or dual, to be more precise.

The Kombi by this time had only two occupants—Donna, who had come into our circle, and me. The two of us decided to head west. The journey was haphazard. We would stop off on the side of the road, occasionally a caravan park, in fields, usually at sites recommended by other travellers in similar vehicles and circumstances. The serviced sites allowed us to wash ourselves and our clothes. They also provided venues that did not provoke the ire of locals or farmers—another perk of the facility.

One day we piled up the van with food, drink and petrol and set off. We eventually pulled into a sheltered lay-by, where Donna and I made a full fledged assault on some cider. This turned out to be a potentially lethal local brew, which led to a loosening of tongues, inhibition and, eventually, clothing. I assume what occurred was mutual, but my reliability as a witness by this time was questionable. I don't even know if I had heard Jimi Hendrix.

What I can recall was the outstanding quality of the sex. It is hard to say where and when mutuality and selfishness blurred. I can remember overhearing Donna once telling another woman at a farm where we stopped to get some scrumpy that while she felt some kind of affection for me, she feared I had a streak of brutality and that, despite her using the contraceptive pill, led to her harbouring an ongoing fear of pregnancy.

As I say, my recall of carnal events is exemplary. Why is it that such details should stand out when so much else around them is lost? It was viscous: our bodies slid on and over and in and out of each other. Abandon was total. Perhaps it was the recovery of privacy—no audience, no competition, no distraction. The only experience comparable—and I fear this is blasphemous—is the abandon one can encounter in contemplative prayer.

Why I could not accept the gift I had been given is a question that confronts me even to today. In our exhaustion on the rug by the van, I saw Donna's buttocks, catching the moonlight. I felt myself harden and rolled on top of her. Her acquiescent murmur—she probably expected me to mount her from behind—turned into a squeal of pain as I pushed into her arse. The tightening muscles, the gasp, the mixture of pleading and reasonability in the statement, 'That really hurts', only served to augment my excitement. For a moment I thought to overcome all resistance. Then I realised that I was on the edge of being—I was—that brute Donna had mentioned. With some regret I withdrew and spilled my seed onto the ground. It was one of the most exciting orgasms I have ever experienced.

Shame strikes me when I find, after all these years of monastic life, that I cannot erase the clarity of the event or the conflicting urges of that moment. I have never felt so overwhelmed with passion, despite the drink. Or perhaps because of it. I was dripping with sweat and exultation. I heard Donna whimpering. I lay to one side, stroking her back and kissing her ear, whispering sincere apologies. I did this for some time. Then I rolled over and went to sleep.

I did not hear Donna get up. I did not hear her dress, pack up her things, or her dump a few of my belongings next to my snoring form. I did not hear the Kombi's engine turn over, its gearbox engage, the roll of wheels and the vehicle depart. I was insensate to everything. I did not really hear the voices that cajoled me, the reassurances that accompanied lifting me up and plonking me into a wheelbarrow, and pushing me to the Guest Wing of the Community of Saint Candida.

The Bearable
Lightness of Being

One idle afternoon, I took up the pile of jottings from my room and read over some of the pages as I sat silently with Fr Aidan. I get a sense of sadness in so much of what I have given myself over to. Not that it has been sad—or even solemn—but if someone were to scan these pages, I fear their impression would be that they have been the recollection of an unhappy man.

Quite the contrary. St Candida's, especially in my novice years, was full of fun. And forgiveness. So much of my ill-spent past I laid to rest. Wise Novice Masters, priests and Fr Abbot ensured we confronted our shortcomings and failures. And helped us to put them behind us. That can only bring joy.

Laughter, jokes, sometimes silliness bordering on insubordination, was key. Brother Cyril, who came to us from his family fruit stall, was full of banter. In his years peddling fruit and vege at Chrisp Street market he developed a lively sense of the absurd. He had a repertoire of impossible Cockney expressions that he applied to our work and life. Within a month of his arrival, each of the brethren had a nickname, used only by Cyril, Matthew—of whom more later—and me.

Cyril was naturally subversive: witty, contrary and delighting in routines of his own making. He had been involved in the serving team of his local church and knew more about Christian doctrine than he let on. He was superb in the sanctuary. He had been drilled in reverential regimentation and possessed an outlook that made him an asset in liturgy: always alert, anticipating the moves and moods of the celebrant, quick to counter any oversight or cover any glitch.

Cyril—his name in the world was Frank—was truly of the world. While deeply prayerful, camouflaged in seemingly vapid rabbitting, he was never really at home in the cloister, even though some thought him the perfect novice. He missed the rush of the city. He went back to Poplar and rejoined the family stall. We received Christmas cards from him, usually with some short scribbled 'news', each year: the changes in populations, the redevelopment of the docks, the push of the supermarkets, the struggle to sell his stock. In the late 1990s he wrote to tell us he was moving out—Suffolk or Essex, I can't remember which—having packed in fruit and vege for security work.

I believe for some time he was Churchwarden to his local church. (Before the move.) I can imagine his mixture of practicality, rootedness in the place in which he had grown up, his easy-going conversation, not to forget his purposeful piety, would have made him a cornerstone and strong support to clergy in such a setting.

The cards stopped coming. Addresses were kept by the Abbot and Fr Aidan had begun to lose the acuity he had formerly given to such clerical work. Where he is, as is Cyril's contribution to CSC, is lost.

Matthew, in a like and different way, was a graphic joker. He took to sketching members of the community—fellow novices at first, (that was, of course, Cyril, Matthew himself and me). These started as mere whimsical renderings of what we did on a daily basis: in the chapel, at our lectures (Matthew had a particular gift for capturing the look of perplexity or confusion on my face during introductory talks on the religious life), meditation (Cyril nodding off). These extended to other members of the community at prayer, work or recreation.

His ability to render a likeness with some inherent commentary, usually with a sense of whimsy, was remarkable. This led to further insights—perhaps a view of us trying to eat some meal that had caused merriment in the Refectory. These small vignettes would be hidden for us in our office books and random volumes in the library. Muted giggles would break the silence of readers when a fellow novice would come across one of Matthew's cartoons. I believe one of the Trustees, while looking over the library before the disposal of the books, came across such a work in a long unopened commentary on 1 Chronicles. I hope it was saved: Matthew's drawings are now selling for far more than could be gained from the academic's analysis of the exploits of King David.

Matthew took to cartooning as a career and was for a long time almost a fortnightly feature in Private Eye. I was told this by a number of visitors who used to quip that PE was a foundation stone of their spiritual reading. I believe his works still appear there from time to time even now.

For all the laughter, lightness and humour, so much seems to pass me by now. Whether it is my personality, background or the grind of life in a monastery, I don't know.

I meet other monastics from time to time and they do not

seem to have lost their lightness of touch. Perhaps the beauty of our surroundings, the diminution of our number—not a singular fault of CSC by any means—and the direction of travel of society. (It would be unfair of me, an arguable misfit, to reflect on what seemed the doubtful quality of potential novices: no longer the brightest and best; more of the mad, bad and dangerous.) Perhaps it is God's way of reminding us, as the Psalmist suggests, that our belief that our names will last forever is delusory.[1]

Which seems to be a long way from thinking about the lighter times of the Novitiate.

1. This would seem to be a reference to Psalm 49, though the translations into English are substantially different. The closest to Br Columba's allusion would be the Authorised Version.

Lazarus House,
Sussex

Dear Fr Scully,

I know you are comfortable with people using your Christian name but, as we at CSC always preferred to maintain honorifics, especially as they seem to be clear-felled in the world around us, I do so now.

I have appreciated your repeated overtures in seeking to re-visit the House. While you would be most welcome here again, I fear even Sussex has greater attractions for you beyond a collection of crumbling clergy, some wives and husbands, and their concession to me as the token monk.

I also appreciate your repeated attempts to return my papers. As I have said before, they are really of no consequence to me. Indeed, they are something of an embarrassment. Especially now you know something of my background. I am sorry I did not respond to the time you mentioned the Central Coast but, to be honest, I was slightly embarrassed. I am sorry if you felt I was holding back on matters we could have spoken of.

As to the papers…such an egotistical pastime was, I have come to realise, an attempt to deal with my circumstances at Care Home which, through no fault of anyone, was quite a solitary life.

Here at Lazarus House I have found my way into a new form of community. It presents its challenges—the ecclesiastical breadth of the residents being only one. I know we are always claiming the diversity of Anglican polity is one of its defining charms or strengths, but the reality is often far from what the politicians call spin. Sometimes it is hard even to imagine how this has been maintained. (If it has; I sometimes fear bishops and other 'leaders' have to sing from a score that they do not really believe!)

But I digress. All this is a far cry from the matter in hand. I appreciate the offer but I really do not want the papers back. As I have said, they were attempts by me to deal with circumstances that are no longer part of my now. The monk's task is to engage with the here and how, while keeping an eye on eternity—for us, our homeland is in heaven, as it says in the epistle to the Philippians[1]—but we need to be where we are. My scribblings were, I suppose, a way of placing the past into the present at Care Home. But things are different here.

The round of public offices, the celebration of Holy Communion and other aspects of our corporate life here provide me with more 'nowness' than I could eke out in Bethnal Green. That part of my journey needs to be as autumn leaves, cast off from the tree that is Columba. The tree metaphor holds well. My roots, while relatively shallow, are in good soil here. The House has a tradition that, like all else, seeks to engage with the past, draws on the present, but with an eye to the future. That means change, of course, with all its attendant thrills and trepidation. They are the leaves of the present spring.

To the papers again: really, please do with them as you wish. My only request is this: if you seek to publish them, as would appear your implicit, if not fully worked out, intention, do not press ahead until I have the opportunity to have finished my work and journey here. This will not be long. My mental faculties remain clear but the toxic cocktail inside my body (St Francis's brother ass) suggests we are nearing its terminus. I have explained to the Master here (and he respects my decision) that I do not want many pharmaceutical, surgical or general medical interventions that will drag out this final act. So let me go and go in peace. As Hopkins wrote,

I have desired to go
   Where springs not fail,
To fields where flies no sharp and sided hail
   And a few lilies blow.[2]

I have no evidence—or is it more a wish?—that this will not be too far off other than what I encounter in my own body. Yet it is best to be realistic. But all this is, of course, in the hand of God.

I also realise some of my writings contain what are very personal matters. I leave you to be the judge as to their suitability. Nothing in them—good, bad, indifferent, sinful— has not been taken to God in an appropriate way. I hope you understand my meaning. I have had the benefit of some fine confessors and spiritual directors in my life, and I am glad to say there are a number of very fine priests here.

My thoughts and prayers continue for you in your ministry. Bethnal Green is a place of relentless change, I know, but there are points of stability which the Church, through you (though you may not feel this) provides. I know your weekly services at Care Home are valued—they certainly were by me—and the round of offices and mass that make up the life Catholic in St Matthew's. Thank God for them. They are the bedrock of our lives.

My best wishes to all at the Sunday service. They really are a jolly bunch, perhaps a little too much so for someone who spent so long in the cloister. I do hope my (to you) understandable reserve was not construed as a sneering standoffishness. As you know, it was—it is—the Blessed Sacrament I came for, and each gathering to celebrate Christ in our midst has its own character.

In all, I hope you and I are, with the saints living and departed, trying to live our lives in praise to the Almighty in an effort to join, rather than be just surrounded by, the Cloud of Witnesses.[3]

Pray for me as I pray for you.

Best wishes,

Columba CSC

1. Philippians 3.20

2. From *Heaven Haven, A Nun Takes the Veil* by Gerard Manley Hopkins. The poem has one other quatrain:

And I have asked to be

Where no storms come,

Where the green swell is in the havens dumb,

And out of the swing of the sea.

3. Columba is referring to Hebrews, Chapter 12.

EDITOR'S NOTE

A round of parochial duties—stewardship campaign, a run of funerals, and a series of visits which led to the dinners and discussions that make up Marriage Preparation, and the normal rota of services—meant that I had slipped in my efforts to put Columba's papers in a proper order to my satisfaction, and a hoped-for approval by him. I had sought a number of times to find the right placement, but never settled on a convincing way of compiling his narrative. That was not just because of the random nature of his notes and the impressionistic sense that was gained from them. There seemed to be a sense of something missing, an ending perhaps. So it was that the task was neither clear nor urgent. I suppose in some ways it does not matter.

Or so I thought until I opened I opened my email programme one morning to find a communication from the Master of Lazarus House, Sussex.

> Dear Fr Scully,
> I email with the news that Brother Columba of the Community of St Candida died suddenly, yet peacefully, in his sleep on Monday. As it happens, I have discovered, it was on the anniversary of his profession. What an irony God has at times.
> As Master it was my privilege and duty to minister the sacraments of the Church to Br Columba during his time here, and particularly to anoint him during his final illness.
> It has now fallen to me to oversee his funeral arrangements. As you know, Bishops' diaries are the

driving force of much in these matters. The Buddhist community now based at the former monastery has been very accommodating in granting access to the cemetery. Columba is to be the last interment there.

The arrangements, thus far, are for the Bishop of Salisbury to say a Requiem Mass at Whitchurch Canonicorum (near Bridport I believe) and commit Columba's mortal remains at the Community cemetery.

Columba was not a great one for idle conversation, as I am sure you learned in your visits to him in London and here. He did, however, ask me to send you his Office Book, his Bible and prayer rope, which I will forward by recorded delivery. He left precious little else. His clothes, few as they were, have been disposed of. He will be buried in his habit and scapular.

I do hope you can come. We will be holding a service here for the residents (I am hoping our Visitor will officiate) who cannot make the journey to Dorset, which is quite a distance, especially if done in the one day.

Best wishes,

Bishops' diaries being the driving force, I was not able to attend. I was approached to conduct at a funeral of parishioner—a resident of Care Home, as it happened—undertakers playing their usual game of making all the arrangements without consulting the clergy beforehand. I found myself oddly distracted during the service, almost to the point of saying Columba's name at the Commendation when I should have said Clifford. Other duties likewise prevented me from taking the train to Sussex to join them.

The promised parcel duly arrived. I had hoped for a well-worn Office book of the community, of archival interest, only to be reminded that CSC had formally adopted the use of *Common Worship* Daily Prayer before they left Dorset. Tucked into the back of the Bible—a tatty Authorised Version which, from the evidence on the endpapers, had been the schoolboy Columba's on the Central Coast of New South Wales—was a birth certificate. His name was Barry Mortimer. No middle name. Part of him was, in part at least, a Londoner, like Father Aidan, albeit from south of the water. No-one, as far as I knew, was aware of his English origins. Unless, of course, anyone besides myself had read his scribblings.

This has left me with a narrative dilemma. In not attending to the papers with the focus they warranted, or indeed with the urgency I should have given them, I have been overtaken by events. I now have to wrestle not with the order so much as tenses. Do I go back and correct what was in the present to the preterite? Can one play with time? When I began this sorting Columba was alive and, thus from my point of view, so was his story. Yet the fact remains that he is no longer. He has gone to meet the maker he so tellingly wrote of. Has that moved his life from the present to the past? Or can I attempt to cast his words in the light of his faith in eternal life—a life that is changed, not taken away?

I have spent some days looking over my notes. They are inevitably sometimes a distraction from other tasks, though this seems a worthy one, too. At times I have sought to elucidate some obscurity or lost practice for the general reader. But what comes through again and again with this man's life's mission was a sense of discontented satisfaction. There was always more to him than could be read. His silence was a shield as well as way of life.

As I sit here at my desk, musing on his writings, I am drawn to making the kind of assessments he made of himself. Has my life been up to the mark? Has my living been commensurate with my preaching? Can people see the light of God in me? Or this too just vanity? Another grasping after an egotistical shadow?

EDITOR'S NOTE

I put down my pen there. For a few days I could not address this material. My days seemed tinged with a wash of senselessness. I was about to call my spiritual director when I realised I had a gap in my diary, so I took myself off to the nearby Priory for a couple of quiet days. There, in my guest room, like one of those overseen by Columba, I spent time in sleep, prayer and reading over his words.

What would be achieved in re-editing what has been something of a labour, not so much of love, as a seeming duty? And yet duty is a driver that must be part of the religious life: we are bound to proclaim the freedom given us. That God's love for us is inexhaustible, even when we have spent all we have for ourselves. There is a perplexing conundrum here. Do people need to be told what should be obvious? After all, we are less walking advertisements as embodiments of faith. Or so we hope.

I am still troubled about the nature of some of Brother Columba's revelations. Maybe I should have sought to discuss them with him. In the papers he speaks of his ill-spent past being laid to rest with gifted confessors and spiritual directors. The seal of the confessional can be on both sides of the grille. For all that, there seems a tinge of unfinished business (perhaps just for me) about some of the events he writes of. But, I suppose, that is so in all our spiritual lives.

So it is in the spirit of the man that I pass on Columba's writings. He has bequeathed an insight—a particular one, it has to be said—about the dying element of monasticism in our church's life. With the latest trends, as with any such developments, new minds believe themselves neologists.

Whereas it is usually a trend, a rebrand. Karl Marx seems to have more to offer to me than theology in understanding the change in church culture.

'Society is undergoing a silent revolution, which must be submitted to, and which takes no more notice of the human existences it breaks down than an earthquake regards the houses it subverts. The classes and the races, too weak to master the new conditions of life, must give way.'[1]

The explosion of contained middle class emotionalism, the beguilingly hip blandness of the songs/hymns, now rebranded worship, the long heaped up phrases of prayer, the extended sermons constitute much of the emerging church's takeover. In this is expressed a naïveté bordering on egomania. Ignorance is the new knowledge. Yet old must give way to new.

Perhaps I need to let stand what I have done. Abandon that, like the life of the men who gave themselves to God in Dorset, to the judge of us all. That is, after all, the real vocation. To let the one who created us deal with his makings.

I intend to visit the cemetery in Dorset. The robed Buddhists, as the Master had told me, are enormously helpful, even to the point offering me accommodation in their guest wing if I want to make an overnight stay.

My wife has suggested we slot it into a bit of a holiday— she is always more adept in combining advantage with duty than I—as we have not spent much time in that part of the country. I can envisage cream teams, ancient sites, country walks and a visit to Columba's grave.

At times it feels that the kind of religious practice I serve has had its day, particularly in London where a new franchise is flexing its muscles into the mainstream. To quote my first insertion, 'Some aspects of them are possibly shocking but, as a fellow Christian (and an Australian-born one at that), I believe Columba's disjointed narrative points to a truth about ourselves—no matter how unpleasant events, experience or thoughts are, they are facts of life. To attempt to alter them would be dishonest. I offer them because they chronicle something of the dying landscape of the Church of England in the early part of the twenty-first century.'

Like Columba, perhaps all I can do is quietly keep walking in the path I set out when I arrived in London at the end of the Australian Bicentennial Year in 1988. God knows I could learn from his example.

1. From an article in *New York Daily Tribune*, March 22, 1853, at least according to Wikiquote.

Acknowledgements

The bulk of Scripture quotations are from **New Revised Standard Version Bible**, copyright © 1989 National Council of the Churches of Christ in the United States of America. Used by permission. All rights reserved.

Revised Standard Version of the Bible, copyright © 1946, 1952, and 1971 National Council of the Churches of Christ in the United States of America. Used by permission. All rights reserved.

Holy Bible, Today's New International Version, Copyright © 2002 by International Bible Society. Used by permission of Hodder & Stoughton Publishers, A member of the Hodder Headline Group. All rights reserved. 'TNIV 'is a registered trademark of International Bible Society.

Scripture quotations from **The Authorized (King James) Version**. Rights in the Authorized Version in the United Kingdom are vested in the Crown. Reproduced by permission of the Crown's patentee, Cambridge University Press.

Extracts from **The Book of Common Prayer**, the rights in which are vested in the Crown, are reproduced by permission of the Crown's patentee, Cambridge University Press.

The author acknowledges the use of extracts from **Common Worship**, © The Archbishops' Council, 2000.